MW00475712

You & Me Make Three

Barrington Billionaire's Series

Book Three

by
Jeannette Winters

Author Contact

website:
JeannetteWinters.com

email:
authorjeannettewinters@gmail.com

Facebook:
Author Jeannette Winters

Twitter:
JWintersAuthor

Shaun Henderson learned young that the best defense is to strike first. It's perfect in business but not in matters of the heart.

Morgan Pereira had walked away from a high-profile position to protect her son. Years later she is given another opportunity to climb the corporate ladder.

Taking the job opens wounds Morgan thought had healed.

If Shaun really does want her, he'll have to learn that some things can't be forced. Love plays by its own rules.

Copyright

Dedication

This book is dedicated to Tyler Dolbec, a special young man who is dear to my heart. Tyler, you taught me love can be expressed in many ways. Thank you.

I am also supported by a team of beta readers who aren't afraid to tell me the truth. Thank you for that!

Karen Lawson, Janet Hitchcock, E.L. King and Marion Arche, my editors you are all amazing!

To my readers who brings joy into my life with each and every message. Always make time for romance

Chapter One

HAVE I LOST my mind? What was I thinking to speak to him like that? Just because he was rude as hell to me, I should've known better than to let him under my skin, telling him to take his job and his uniform and shove them. Morgan sat on the stone bench by the water fountain. The pigeons came up to her feet, looking for something to eat. She threw them a few more pieces of popcorn, and they all fought over it.

She'd been working at that same café for a few years as a barista, and until that morning, she'd actually liked her job. When the new manager came and handed her the new uniform, she knew things were about to go bad. Just because the other girls didn't have the courage to question his rational on this choice of clothing didn't mean she didn't. Besides it was her reputation on the line. There was no way she was wearing shorts that barely covered her bottom and a T-shirt that was two sizes too small, leaving nothing to the imagination.

Her first attempt to veto the clothing had been shot down completely. When she told him she refused to dress like that, she couldn't believe he had the nerve to tell her if she couldn't use her assets to their best ability for the company, then he would find another hottie to take her place. *When did I stop being a person and become only an . . . object?*

"Looks like I'll be joining you and begging soon because I have no idea how I'm going to pay rent with no job."

"You don't need to work for a jerk like that."

Morgan turned to find a blonde sitting not far from her. She looked familiar—one of the regulars who came in—but had she been one of the customers in the shop when Morgan decided to tell her boss what he could do with that uniform? It had gone by so fast, who had been there seemed to be a blur.

"Sorry, do I know you?"

The woman held out her hand. "My name's Lexi Chambers. I have to say, I was very impressed with how you handled that jerk. Can't say I wasn't disappointed that you didn't slap his face, because he sure had it coming."

I don't need assault charges on top of being unemployed. "Thanks, I'm Morgan Pereira."

"So, what are you going to do now?" Lexi asked.

Get some chocolate chip ice cream, sit here, and cry if you don't mind. That wasn't going to make anything better at this point, but her options seemed bleak. Going back to apologize was not on the list. No matter how desperate she was for work, she had standards. *It's not the first job I've had to leave unexpectedly, but I hope it'll be the last.* "Look for a new job."

"Well, then this is your lucky day."

Morgan had to fight back a sarcastic remark. Nothing about today felt lucky, but this woman was grinning from ear to ear. Was she crazy or had she not heard everything that went down a few minutes earlier?

She turned away from her and started feeding the pigeons again. *Maybe if I don't look at her, she'll go away.* No such luck.

"Come with me."

"Excuse me?" *This woman must have a screw loose.*

"I just heard you tell your boss off, and he was almost a foot taller than you, so you can't tell me that you're afraid of me?"

Lexi might have a point, but that wasn't enough to make Morgan get up and follow her without even a clue as to where they were going. Although she looked harmless, this was Boston, and it was filled with some very questionable individuals. Morgan didn't want to make her bad day any worse.

"I'm just going to sit here."

"And do what? Grow old feeding pigeons? Come on. Best time to get a job is while you have one."

"And I don't."

Lexi shook her head. "A technicality. It's still the same day, so it's almost like you have a job."

Morgan arched her brow, trying to figure out her logic. There was none. Before she could correct her, Lexi smiled.

"Just go with it. Now if you want a job, I know a place that needs someone to start today. You'd be perfect. So are you interested or not?"

"What place is that, and how do you know they're hiring?"

"Poly-Shyn, and I work there."

Morgan knew the place as it was only around the corner from the café and many of the employees came there regularly. She never imagined she'd work there. But from the looks of Lexi, she wasn't sure she believed Lexi worked there now. Everyone there always dressed the same: dark suit, plain tie. Boring as the day is long.

"In the office?" Morgan couldn't help but be skeptical. The Hendersons were known for taking business to an entirely different level. She couldn't picture Lexi fitting into that world, not with her personality.

Lexi stood proudly. "Yes, the office. I work in Human Resources, and I know they are looking for someone to start today."

Wow. A foot in the door at a place like that is nearly impossible to come by. But I am not qualified to work in HR. That department works under federal and state standards. Why would I waste my time going for a job that there is no chance I'd get? "Thank you, Lexi. That is very kind of you, but I have no HR experience at all. It really doesn't matter what your department is hiring for. I don't have the necessary skill set." *Not that I couldn't learn, but why would they hire me when there are so many people who already have the skills needed to do the job correctly right out of the gate. Damn it. Why can't I just bullshit my way through an interview like other people? What does ethical behavior really get me? Oh yeah, I know. Unemployed.*

"Trust me. You have what it takes."

What is that? She already knows I make an awesome cup of coffee. I don't think that will get me past day one there. "You don't know me, Lexi."

"I saw you in action, remember? You have balls, and that's what you need to work for Dean Henderson. Actually, any Henderson, for that matter."

Not a great sales pitch if you are trying to sell me on coming to Poly-Shyn with you. "I just left working for a chauvinistic jerk. I don't need another one."

Lexi laughed. "He's many things, but chauvinistic is not one of them. Trust me; Tessa has softened him up a lot. Well maybe a little bit would be more accurate. So what do you say? You want a job or not?"

What's the saying? Beggars can't be choosers? I need the money. Even if I only last a week, it will be better than nothing. What do I have to lose? Getting up, Morgan forced a smile.

"Lead the way."

Lexi gave her a quick hug and said, "Morgan, you're a lifesaver."

Shouldn't I be saying that to her? This doesn't sound good. A company like that cannot or should not be desperate for staff. I wonder what's really going on. As they made their way around the block, the tall glass building was in sight. No one could miss the name Henderson on the building. They were one of the most powerful families on the East Coast. Walking in there, totally unprepared for any type of interview, was absolutely ludicrous. No way in hell was she going to get hired for a job. *They will take one look at me and the way I'm dressed and throw me out on my butt where I belong.*

Morgan stopped outside the building and looked up. It would be amazing to work in such a remarkable place. The building stood out architecturally from the others close by. Having a name like that on her résumé would open doors. *Not that I want to join that competitive back-stabbing work force again. It's not my dream job, but I know many people who'd kill for an opportunity like this.* There was no time to live in a fantasy world of what her dream job would be. Responsibilities kept her rooted to the ground, and in just a few minutes Lexi had her head in the clouds. *How did she do that? I'm no pushover, so what am I doing here with her?*

She turned to go back in the direction they had come. *Oh yeah. Looking for work.*

Lexi must have sensed her hesitation. Reaching out, she grabbed Morgan's hand and half dragged her into the building. The man dressed in a security uniform looked at her puzzled, then raised his hand to halt them from going forward.

Damn it. She might not even work here. Oh God. I'm being dragged along by some woman pretending to be an employee. I knew it from the moment I saw her outfit. How stupid could I be to actually believe her?

"Miss Chambers. You know you can't bring in a guest without stopping here and showing proper identification," the man said before they could pass him.

Lexi turned to Morgan. "Do you have your license with you?"

Morgan nodded and pulled it out of her purse. Lexi looked at it first, then back to her. "What?"

"You're thirty-six? I would've thought twenty-eight. You're going to need to give me your secret before I leave."

Not working a high stress job like the one you're taking me to interview for. But I'm not worried. There's no way they are going to hire me dressed like this. God knows I wouldn't if I were in their shoes.

Lexi handed the card to the man who entered the information into the computer and handed her a temporary badge.

"And what's your business here today?"

"She's here to see Dean," Lexi replied.

Dean? Dean Henderson? The owner of Poly-Shyn?

"Lexi . . ." Morgan began.

"Okay. You better make it quick. He just asked for the limo to pull up as he and his brother Shaun are heading out," the guard reported.

"This will only take a minute. Thanks." Lexi grabbed Morgan's hand once again and pulled her to the elevators.

Once inside Morgan asked again, "Lexi, you can't honestly be taking me to meet the owner of the company. I'm not prepared, and up until a few hours ago, I worked in a café making specialty coffees for people who work here, for goodness sake. Besides, I know there is a protocol for such a thing. I mean, you're in HR. You should know that. Wouldn't I meet your department first to see where I fit best?"

It wasn't that she didn't want the opportunity, but making a fool of herself wasn't what she was looking for. People like the Hendersons had a long memory. This family wasn't one she wanted knowing her name, especially if it was on bad terms.

"Morgan, I told you, they need someone to start today. Trust me. They will love you."

If they love coffee, then yes. If they want someone with a college degree in HR Management, then the answer is no. "And you know this how?"

"Dean and I have been friends for years. And I'm a good judge of character. So stop sweating it."

The elevator doors opened, and they made their way down the hall. She saw an empty secretarial desk beside a closed door. This scene would normally tell a person to stop and wait for the person in charge to return, but she watched Lexi walk around the desk and knock on the door anyway. When no one answered, she knocked again.

Really? And you keep this job how? Morgan wanted to turn and head back where she came from, but before she could a tall man who looked like he should be on a cover of GQ opened the door. She knew from recent news photos that this wasn't Dean, but whoever he was, he was delicious to look at. Morgan averted her eyes so not to get caught staring. *You're here regarding a professional position, so act like you are professional, Morgan.*

"Wow. You learned to knock. I'm impressed."

Lexi shot him a dirty look. "Very funny, Shaun. Hey, can you do me a favor?"

He looked at her long and hard before answering her. "Probably not."

Lexi then pointed to Morgan, who stood quietly to the side. "I need you to keep her company while I go talk to Dean for a minute. She's a new employee here, so don't scare her away."

Shaun looked her over from head to toe. It wasn't in a sexual way, but much more critical. She couldn't help but feel uncomfortable. He wasn't the owner, so whoever he was, he was full of himself. If it wasn't that she still held the slightest hope that she might land the position, she would've given him a piece of her mind. *Come this far, might as well go for the gold.*

"Make it quick. I have better things to do," Shaun said to Lexi, but his eyes still were fixed on Morgan.

She turned away to avoid any conversation with him. From the look in his eyes, it wouldn't be pleasant. The way her day was going she wasn't sure how she'd be at holding her tongue. Even the pleasantry of an introduction was more than she wanted with him. *The less you know the better.*

Morgan sat down and hoped Lexi was correct, and she would only be sitting there a few minutes. *How she's going to talk him into an interview in that short of time is beyond me. But she's a fast talker. He'll probably do it just to shut her up.* Morgan tried to hide the grin that crossed her face as she pictured Dean sitting behind his desk being railroaded until he gave in. *Lexi really needs to change jobs and get into contract negotiations. The competition would raise the white flag of surrender for sure.*

Chatting with customers, whether they were strangers or not, was her livelihood. This man somehow made her uncomfortable. She wasn't sure why, but maybe it was the way he continued to watch her. Out of the corner of her eye, she saw him sitting to the right of her and bluntly staring.

Didn't your mother ever teach you any manners? Staring is not polite. Morgan couldn't take it. After the morning she had, she wasn't about to cut anyone any slack.

"Is there something you want to say?"

He arched a brow before asking, "Do I know you?"

If he'd come into the café, she never would've forgotten. He might be bold and brash, but he was also sexy as hell. He was clean-shaven, and dressed in what she could only assume to be a high-end designer suit. One might mistake him for dry and serious, but something in his dark eyes said he had just the right amount of bad boy in him. *The type of man you dream of at night.*

"No."

"Lexi said you work here. Doing what exactly?"

That's a great question. Remind me to ask that next time I see her. Morgan wasn't about to let on to how she came to be in this office. It was none of his business. If he was the owner, that might be a different story, but coworkers had no need for such information.

"If you have any questions regarding my employment, please speak to Mr. Henderson." *That is if I even have a job.*

Before Shaun could respond to her the door opened again, and Lexi came out but this time followed by a man she'd seen before. Dean Henderson was well known after being shot in this very building a few months ago. He looked even more intimidating in person than he did in the newspapers.

Pull yourself together. You've made it this far. Don't let him see the fear or you won't have a chance at whatever it is Lexi has planned.

"Morgan, this is Dean. I've explained to him what happened today at your job and what an ass your boss was. He's agreed to give you a week to prove yourself."

And so much for keeping my private life private. And from the little I've seen of you, Lexi, I can only picture how you embellished it too. She could only do one thing, show her new boss some gratitude for this opportunity.

"Thank you, Mr. Henderson. I really appreciate this."

"Not like I have much of a choice." He looked her

over and shook his head. Obviously, her appearance was not what he was expecting. Turning back to Lexi, he continued. "Lexi, if this doesn't work out, you'll be hearing from Tessa."

Lexi didn't seem worried at all. How she was able to stand between two powerful, scary looking men and not seem to be fazed one bit blew her mind. Morgan hoped whatever her job was going to be, that it wouldn't have much interaction with either of them. *I don't want to be in the spotlight or in the line of fire, and that is exactly where Lexi is standing.*

"Dean, trust me. Am I ever wrong? I mean look at Willa and Lance. Did you ever think—?"

"No Lexi. You didn't think. That's the problem," Shaun interrupted.

For the first time, Morgan saw the light in Lexi's eyes dim just a bit. *Who are Willa and Lance? And did you get them jobs too?*

Lexi didn't stay down long before she was shooting back with more names. "Well, how about Dean and Tessa?"

Lexi seemed to be enjoying the banter back and forth, but Morgan didn't want to get involved in any drama, and that is exactly what this sounded like.

Shaun laughed, but Morgan knew it was more sarcastic than anything. "Oh, taking credit for that too?"

Lexi put her hands on her hips and said, "Shaun Henderson, laugh now, but watch out or I might just decide you're next on my list."

Then she winked at Morgan, who was baffled by the entire exchange. *What am I walking into?* She tried giving her a warning look, but Lexi seemed oblivious to it. *Don't you dare drag me into this, whatever this is. All I want is a job, nothing more.*

Shaun looked from Lexi to Morgan and became serious once again. "Lexi, you can play with others if you want, but I am warning you, stay out of my life. I am not as forgiving as you might think."

"All bark, Shaun, and you know it."

Shaun stared at her and said, "Play your game with me, Lexi, and I guarantee you won't like what you find." Then he turned to Dean and said, "I've got some calls to make. We'll do lunch another time."

Dean nodded as Shaun left the waiting area. Now with just the three of them there she hoped to get some answers.

"Thank you, Mr. Henderson, for the—"

"Don't thank me. If it weren't for Lexi telling me just now that this is her last day, you wouldn't have the job."

Wait. What? Lexi quit. Is that the job I am taking? Hers?

Dean didn't stand around. Instead he brushed past them both, heading in the same direction Shaun had. *The Henderson reputation seems to hold true. They are not to be messed with.* Now alone with Lexi, Morgan was going to get some answers.

"What exactly was that about?"

"Oh, yeah. I just quit my job, but trust me, you'll do

fine. Hey, I didn't know a thing about HR when I started. You'll learn."

Sure, but not in a week, and that's all I have been given. One damn week.

"So let me show you to your desk."

How did I go from a coffee shop to big corporate America in less than thirty minutes? Maybe I should cut back to decaffeinated.

ALTHOUGH SHAUN HAD no intention of meeting up with Dean for lunch, they seemed to arrive in the lobby at the same time.

"What are you thinking, Dean? There is no way that woman has the experience needed to do that job." *She can't even dress for the interview.*

"I know that."

"Then why would you hire her?" Maybe his brother was losing the edge he needed to run Poly-Shyn. Their father had been a hard-ass. Even if you were qualified, he would still toss you out on your ass in a heartbeat for even questioning his instructions. Shaun knew the company couldn't continue in that manner without eventually being sued, but there had to be some middle ground.

"I can't have it all falling on Tessa."

"Call a temp agency. Get someone who looks like they belong in an office."

If Dean had seen Morgan before agreeing to hire her, Shaun would have thought he hired her because she was cute as hell. If he had passed her on the street, he would've given her a second look, maybe even a third. She was average height, but not like one of those women who look like they forgot how to eat. She was curvy in all the right places. *I'd have been almost tempted to overlook her lack of qualifications too. But business is business.*

"It's only a week. It'll give Tessa time to find a replacement. Lexi didn't give us any notice."

"What did you expect? That is who she is. The day you told me she was working for you, I told you to fire her."

"Trust me, I was very tempted, but Tessa said she accurately and promptly did a great job with every task she gave her."

Shaun couldn't picture that. Tessa was so sweet that she probably couldn't bring herself to say anything negative about another person. He, on the other hand, lived in reality, and the truth was Dean and Poly-Shyn were better off without Lexi. They had known her for many years, and responsible was not a word he would've used concerning anything Lexi did. It was only a matter of time before the ripple effect of having her around would have been felt. He'd only heard rumors of what she pulled with the Barringtons, and he sure didn't want any problems like that involving his family.

"Did you even ask Lexi how she knows this woman? Are they friends?" *Because a friend of Lexi's might be as bad as having Lexi.*

"She was vague. All I know was her boss made a

crude remark, and Morgan went off on him."

Shaun laughed. "That's it?" Dean nodded. "You've lost your fucking mind. For all you know she screws shit up, and he had every right to say what he did. What are you going to do when she decides to give you what you have coming? I mean, you might have softened a bit since Tessa came into your life, but you're still a bastard to work for."

Dean shrugged. "If you're so damn worried about it, why don't you keep an eye on her for me? Tessa and I are going to Paris for a week, and I could use someone watching over Poly-Shyn while we are—"

"Ask Brice."

"I did. He said no."

"Okay, how about Zoey, or Alex, or Logan?"

"They all said no."

So I'm your last choice? Damn bro. I'm not sure if I'm hurt you didn't ask earlier or pissed they said no.

He really shouldn't be shocked. Out of everyone in the family, Shaun had worked closest with their father. That wasn't a good thing, as it put an even bigger rift between them. Shaun had learned at a young age how to blend into the background and not to make waves. Maybe that was why his father allowed him to be indirectly involved with Poly-Shyn when he was alive.

All those years, providing investment opportunities, no one knew I was his son. Probably was a good thing. His name didn't open doors; it only got them slammed in his face.

Even now he worried how much of his father he carried inside of him. You don't spend that much time with a person and not absorb something. Since he'd never seen anything good in the man, he knew the trait handed down to him was how to be an asshole.

"So will you do it?"

It only made sense since he was more familiar with the company. Normally he wouldn't bother, even for his brother, but for his soon-to-be sister-in-law he'd do it. "In one week, Dean, you better have your ass back behind that desk."

"Hey, don't think I'm going to be having a grand ole time. Tessa is dragging me out wedding shopping. I tried to get her to go with Zoey or her mother, but she insisted we do this together."

Laughter rumbled through Shaun. "And you were telling me I need to get out and find someone. No thanks, Dean. You can enjoy all this fun by yourself." He shook his head. "If you start picking out colors for dresses don't tell me. I'm not sure I'll be able to handle it."

Dean looked at him, giving a warning glare. "Keep it up, Shaun. I can't wait till it's your turn. You'll probably go around holding her purse or something."

"Don't hold your breath. I'm not about to fall into the trap you and Brice have."

That's exactly what love was. A trap that meant you stopped being who you were and instead jumped through hoops because some woman said so. It didn't matter if they were as attractive as Morgan; he liked his life exactly the way it was.

Twice in one day people are wishing a serious relationship on me. What did I do to piss them all off? And now I get to play babysitter. This week can't get any worse.

Chapter Two

MORGAN HARDLY SLEPT a wink that night. Not only had Lexi provided her with what her responsibilities would be and how to perform them, but she also had a crash course on how to handle a Henderson. That had never been part of an on-the-job training session before. She knew Dean was going to be difficult, but from what she saw, his brother Shaun was worse. *I really need this job, but I'm not sure I can handle reporting to him. The way he looked at me . . . he already doesn't like me. Why? I hadn't even opened my mouth, and he was scrutinizing me.*

She waved to the man behind the security desk and made her way to the elevator. *This whole situation is crazy. Yesterday I was making coffee in a cheesy café. Today I'm working for one of the most influential families in Boston. I wish my old boss could see me now.*

She stepped in and, as the doors closed, she pulled out her compact from her purse. Yesterday she'd had no time to prepare, but today she looked the part. Her long-sleeved white blouse was buttoned to the top; her dark *y* skirt came down to the knee. The only thing she wasn't able to gain full control of was her hair. Although she spent almost thirty minutes forcing each strand into a tight bun, the wind had done a job on it. At times like this she wished she didn't have a mass of unruly curls. There was no way to get them back under control without the proper tools.

She had no choice but to unclip it and let the curls have their way. Morgan bent over shaking her hair and ran her fingers through the strands, hoping to untangle it. "What I'd give for a brush right now. I should know better than to leave home without one."

She hadn't heard the doors open and close again, but out of the corner of her eye she caught movement, then a pair of fine leather shoes came in view, not far from where she was still bent over. *Shit. Not the most flattering position to be in. Please don't be Dean. This is not the way I want him to see me on my first full day.*

Flipping her long hair back over her shoulder, she stood to compose herself and found the other person she was hoping not to see. *Shaun.*

Once again his eyes were fixed on her. He didn't speak; he only took in every inch of her. She could feel the pulse beating in her throat, and it was as though he was enjoying making it race faster. Her earlier actions and now her physical response to him made her cheeks burn. The last thing she wanted was for him to think she was in any way attracted to him. He was not her type. *Arrogant.* But she couldn't deny he was also drop-dead gorgeous. Normally she didn't like facial hair, but his was trimmed neatly and accented his strong jaw even more. Morgan had to stop before she found herself looking him over, just as he was her. Never mind it being unprofessional, it also wasn't ladylike.

However, all she could manage was, "What are you doing here?"

He didn't respond. His eyes darkened to almost black, and he intensified his gaze on her. If he was trying to intimidate her, it was working. She stepped backward until her back was against the elevator wall. She pulled her eyes from his and tried to look anywhere but at him.

Why aren't we moving? Is the elevator stuck or something? That's when she noticed no buttons were lit on the control panel. *Helps if I press a button and tell it where to go.* There was no way she was going to get to the fourth floor unless she got the courage to brush past him and actually press the darn button.

"Don't you have someplace to be?" Shaun asked as though he knew her plight.

"If you don't mind, could you please press four for me?" Her voice was soft as she spoke. She wasn't afraid of him so why was she being so meek and mild now? What was wrong with her? You don't spend years serving the public without building a thick skin. Shaun somehow made her forget that.

"Is there something stopping you from pressing it yourself?"

Other than you being an arrogant ass, yes, your hot

muscular body is. He was right. She was acting like a child. There was no reason why she couldn't reach around him, press the dang button, and be done with it. *Except I don't trust my legs not to give way. He's just a man. It's not like I haven't been around a million of them. I just need to press the damn button and get my butt to work before Dean has a reason to fire me on my first day.*

Stepping forward, she leaned around him and pressed the button for the fourth floor. The elevator started to move. He turned and hit the button for the top floor. During her brief tour yesterday with Lexi she found out there was only one office on that floor and it belonged to Dean. *Off to see your brother again today? Don't you have a job to get to? Oh God. Don't tell me you work for him too. The last thing I want is you as a cowork-er.*

Before either of them could say anything more, the doors opened.

"Excuse me."

He stepped slightly out of her way, but not completely, never taking his eyes off her. Once she moved out of the doors she turned and right before they closed said, "Please tell your brother I'll be up within the hour with the files he needed."

Was it her imagination or was he grinning? It really didn't matter. He most likely would be gone when she was scheduled to meet with Dean for the signatures on the forms Lexi said he would need each Tuesday morning. *If not, he surely won't be as brash in front of others as he was just now.*

Morgan hurried down the hall and started compiling all the documents she needed for her meeting with Dean. Surprisingly, she'd retained enough from yesterday without having to refer to her notes. *Not a bad teacher, Lexi. Not bad at all.*

That wasn't her first impression of Lexi. There were many words she would use to describe her: Spunky. Confident. Absolutely funny as heck. But professional? No.

From her comments, it appeared people didn't take Lexi seriously. Morgan had wanted to say it could be the way she dressed, but it wasn't her place to say such a thing. *Not sure I would say that to my closest friend.* What Morgan could tell, was Lexi was extremely organized, and filling her shoes wasn't going to be an easy task. *Don't judge the book by its cover. I may look the part, but I have no real clue why I am doing what I'm doing. I hope I can last the week without doing too much damage.*

When all the forms were prepared, she stood, ready to get the signatures. Instead, she sat back down and pulled out the hand mirror she'd seen in the desk drawer earlier. There was no way she was going to meet with Dean looking unkempt. It was a great look for a night out on the town, but not how she wanted to be viewed by her boss. Thankfully Lexi had left her what she called a "be ready for anything kit" in the desk drawer. Pulling it out she'd found all the basic toiletries and a few not so basic. Morgan smiled. *Interesting girl, but I have to say, she's prepared for anything.*

She was relieved to find a brush and once again force the curls to behave. It was no easy task, but after several minutes she had them under as much control as she could. One last look in the mirror and her confidence had returned. *Yes. I've got this.*

Smiling, she picked up the files and made her way to see the boss man himself. *Please let this go smoothly. I didn't get to speak to him much yesterday. This will be my first chance to show him I'm not only capable of doing this job, but I can look the part too.*

"Hi, you must be Morgan."

"Yes, I am."

The bubbly young secretary, grinning from ear to ear, said, "My name is Brittany-Lynn. Welcome to Poly-Shyn."

Her warm personality filled the room. Morgan liked her already, and it was refreshing not to have another stuffy suit to deal with. *Dean can't be that bad if someone so innocent looking could be on his front line and deal with him all day.* "Thank you, I'm here to see Mr. Henderson."

"He's expecting you. Go right in."

Excellent. Now all I have to do is stay composed and professional then get out of there.

"Good luck," Brittany-Lynn added right before Morgan opened the door.

Those were two words you never want to hear right before entering the lion's den. "Thanks." *I think I'm gonna need it by the look in your eyes.*

At that point, it really didn't matter what she was walking into. She had a job, and that meant everything to her. Not only was it a job, but it was paying twice as much as she was making at the café. No matter how gruff or demanding Dean was, she would suck it up and say *yes sir.*

She knocked on the door and waited.

"Enter."

He was seated behind his desk, his back to her, and he seemed to be on the phone.

"Just do it," he barked.

Nothing like telling instead of asking.

"That's your problem not mine."

Is this what I have to look forward to? Yeah probably. Now I know why his secretary wished me luck. He definitely woke up on the wrong side of the bed.

"Results are all I care about. You deal with the how."

Thank you, Lexi. You failed to mention this. Was it on purpose? As he continued to make his point crystal clear, Morgan's nerves kicked in full force. *Unemployment isn't the worst thing that could've happened yesterday. I would've found another job somewhere. Eventually. Of course, I would have to work two jobs to equal this one. Oh damn. Suck it up. It's his job to be tough. That's what owners of large companies do. And that's why I'll never be one.*

When she saw his hand move from his ear, she prepared herself. She was next in line to deal with his foul mood. Turning in his chair, she faced one frustrated, angry man. One problem. It wasn't Dean.

What the—

"Have a seat."

Shaun. Morgan didn't move. "I have a meeting with De—I mean Mr. Henderson."

"I'm Mr. Henderson," he said, grinning wickedly at her.

Not funny. Not at all. "Your brother. *Not* you."

He leaned back in his chair and once again looked at her in a way that made her self-conscious.

"He didn't tell you." It was more a statement than a question. It was obvious that she had no clue what he was talking about.

"Would you care to explain?" *Not that I really want to be here listening to you, but you seem to be the only option I have right now.*

"Sit."

I'm not a dog you can command to sit. What comes next? Give you my paw? Someone really needs to put you in your place. Although I'm tempted, I think I better find out what's going on first.

Morgan didn't move immediately, but he apparently wasn't going to be forthcoming with any information until she submitted to his demand, so she reluctantly took the seat opposite from the desk. *You don't know how much I hate caving in to you. But you seem to hold all the cards. For now that is.*

"What exactly didn't your brother tell me?"

Shaun became much more serious and sat upright in

his seat. "He's out of the country for a week."

"Okay, then I guess I will reach out to Tessa." Lexi had provided her name and number as the go-to person if Dean was unable to be reached for such things as signatures. *Being his fiancée, she had access to him that others did not.*

"That's not going to be possible."

"And why is that?" Was he trying to throw her off her game? Set her up so she failed on her first day? *Yeah most likely. But guess what? I am more capable than you believe.*

"Tessa is with him," Shaun stated, showing no change in emotion.

No Dean. No Tessa. Lexi didn't provide a plan C. "Well, I guess I . . . I could . . . maybe . . ."

"You should give me the forms, and I'll review and sign them."

She thought at first he was joking. He wasn't on the signature list. *At least, not as far as I know. He's family. Maybe they do this all the time. I don't know their dynamics. Heck, I don't know anything about this family except what I read in the newspaper.*

Shaun reached across the desk waiting for the files. Morgan wasn't sure what to do. Don't give them to him and hold up payroll for the entire facility or hand them over and let him potentially steal his brothers banking information off the ACH transfer documents. *Should I flip a coin? Or in this case, close my eyes and hope for the best. Either I lose my job, or my new coworkers kill me for not being paid. This is a no-win situation. Damn, what a way to start a new job.*

Morgan held her breath, stood up, and said, "I am sorry, but unless you have some form of proof as to your authority to review these documents, I will not be able to share them with you."

Rule number one from Lexi. HR is responsible for the privacy of all personnel information, and that includes payroll. Sorry Shaun, but you're not going to make me break the rules not matter how intensely you look at me.

If she thought he would be angry or challenge her response, she was mistaken. Instead, he dismissed her abruptly.

"If that's the case, I suggest you get back to work. I'll leave you to explain to Dean when he returns next week."

That explanation was surely going to come with a termination if Shaun, in fact, was covering for Dean and Tessa. Morgan got up and headed for the door. Her hand was on the knob, and all she needed to do was turn it, open it, and leave. But she froze.

"Have you changed your mind?"

Thinking. Quit pushing already. Turning to face him, she tried to look as confident as possible. "I'll be back by one and will have my answer then." *How I'm going to determine what to do by then, I have no clue. But I'm not going to be bullied into it. Doesn't mean I won't cave, but at least it will be on my terms, not yours.*

Before he could respond, she opened the door and

left the office. Her heart was pounding as she made her way to the elevator. *Think Morgan. Think hard. Your job and potentially freedom is on the line. You don't want to break protocol, never mind break the law.*

She hated to do it, but she had no choice. Morgan was going to need to call Lexi and hope for an answer. The right one might be asking too much, but at this point, any guidance was better than throwing a dart blindfolded.

SHAUN HAD TO give her credit. Most people would've backed down and handed him the information whether it was against company policy or the law. Morgan may have stood her ground, but he clearly saw panic in her eyes. He knew if he'd pushed her any further she would've crumbled. Yet something in him prevented him from doing so. *Could it have been your whiskey brown eyes that begged me to challenge you? Or that pout that made you almost too hard to resist as you tried to stare me down.*

He ran his fingers through his hair frustrated at the week ahead of him. It really didn't matter what it was. Nothing was going to happen. Shaun had no issue with enjoying a woman's company for a night or two, but anything more than that was out of the question. Some fun with Morgan might just make the potential week from hell worth his trouble. Although she tried to portray a hell of a lot of confidence, he saw something lying beneath it. Was it insecurity or innocence? Normally he would avoid both like the plague, yet on her it looked damn good. *I wonder how you feel about a casual affair?*

He laughed to himself as he recalled Dean telling him she had told off her old boss. What exactly transpired between them hadn't been clear, but it did show she was no pushover. *Too bad. It would make this week a whole lot more interesting.*

Dean failed to mention several things to him with his last minute instructions. What he thought might be minor coverage, in fact, meant reviewing final documents for a deal he'd had on the table. It was a small insignificant deal, yet anytime you dealt with Trent Davis you wanted to double check everything. He might be a friend of their older brother Brice, but when it came to business there was no such word as friend. *Why the hell did I agree to this? I have my own business to run. You might be my kid brother, but you've never listened to my advice before. Asking me to stand in for you now wasn't wise, but now maybe things will get done right around here.*

He looked at the clock. Two minutes before one. Letting the entire staff not get paid while Dean was out of the country might not be the direction to take, but he wasn't going to back down. *A lesson to be learned, Morgan. Don't take a job that you're not prepared for. Especially one with the Hendersons. We're not known for playing nice.*

There was a knock on the door. *I see you came to your senses. Good.* "Come in."

His smug look quickly faded as he saw it was his sister, Zoey. She was dressed in business attire today. From her appearance, she must have scheduled a meeting with Dean and his staff because she never dressed like that unless she had business to attend to.

"Good afternoon, Zoey. Where are you off to dressed like that?"

"Here."

"Dean's away unless you forgot."

She smiled sweetly at him. "I'm not that much older than you; my memory hasn't gone. I just came by to make sure you weren't going to sell the place out from underneath him. I know how much you *love* Poly-Shyn."

It wasn't a secret to anyone about the disdain between him and his late father. No one spoke of it outside the family and rarely mentioned it among themselves. Zoey, on the other hand, never held anything back. She was like a mother hen. Always in your business and appearing out of nowhere. He and his brothers all thought her talents would be much better suited for the Secret Service than meddling in their lives.

Shaun wasn't about to tell her why he'd agreed to help Dean. Actually, he didn't quite know himself. Dean was family, and no matter what differences they had in the past, they would do anything for each other. But he knew that hadn't been his motivation. Not this time at least. *I just want to keep an eye on Morgan. Something's not right there. I just know it.*

"If you're so concerned, maybe you should've said yes when he asked you."

Zoey laughed. "After Dean's little episode with Tim

when he first took over Poly-Shyn, I think I'll keep my name out of the business side. Visiting for lunch dates is as close as you'll ever see me."

Shaun still couldn't believe how far a former employee had been willing to go for what he considered justified payback. Not that he'd ever want to see another member of his family in harm's way again, but never had the family rallied as one before. *Each of us willing to take a bullet for the other.* Even months later, they all watched their backs more than they had in the past.

Zoey had never given another person a reason to hurt her. She was the one person in the family who wasn't an asshole. When he'd asked her one day why she was so different from them, she had the simplest answer. "I'm not. I just choose to be nice each day." *Sweet Zoey. If life only was that damn easy.*

He totally agreed with her reasoning of not having anything to do with this company. If it wasn't Dean pissing people off, their father had had a list of enemies a mile long. The guys grew up with constant threats from their father. There wasn't much more a stranger could do to them. They had all tried to protect Zoey from his wrath. It was still their job now to shelter her from the repercussions of being James Henderson's offspring.

"Understandable. Since it's not meetings or work that brings you here, why the visit?"

"I make it a habit to stop in on Dean and drag him from his desk for lunch each week. With him gone, guess you're going to have to fill in."

Even as children Zoey always felt the need to pay extra attention to Dean. Maybe because he was the baby in the family. *Or maybe because he couldn't stay out of trouble for longer than five minutes.*

"Those aren't shoes I want to fill, Zoey." *Not in any aspect.*

She laughed again. "Oh, you thought I was asking? No, I'm pulling the big sister card and telling you you're taking me to lunch."

He would've laughed if he thought for one minute she was joking. When she had her mind set on something, you could argue with her for hours or just concede right away. *Better if you make it quick and painless. She won't stop until she gets her way.*

Before he could say yes or no there was another knock on the door. *How does Dean get anything done in this damn place with continuous interruptions?*

"Come in."

This time Morgan peeked her head inside. "Sorry, I didn't know you were in a meeting."

Zoey turned her head toward Morgan then back to Shaun. "New employee?"

Shaun waved Morgan in.

Morgan walked up to the desk. He watched her as she scanned Zoey out of the corner of her eye, then angled her face just enough to avoid seeing her altogether. If he didn't know better, he would've thought she was checking out the competition. *Maybe your distaste for me is not as strong as you make it out to be, Morgan.*

Her voice was flat as she spoke to him when she handed him the files from earlier. "The forms are ready for you to sign, Mr. Henderson."

As he took the manila file from her, he didn't hold back the slight grin. "Did you change your mind?"

Shaun loved watching her eyes turn a darker brown as she became angry. He could tell she wanted to say something else, but held her words. Just what he would expect from someone in HR.

"I was able to obtain the information required. If you would be so kind as to sign them, I'll be sure to process them immediately."

While he signed the documents Zoey, in her usual friendly form, wanted to be all warm and fuzzy. He didn't want to break the moment.

"Hi, I'm Shaun's—"

"Lunch date."

Zoey looked at Morgan, then shot him a puzzled look. A smile he knew all too well crossed her lips as she spoke. "Yes, and I'm famished. I can't wait to hear how your day is going."

And she's going to make me pay for this. I should've known better. I don't play games, why the hell am I starting now? I'm not interested in her. This little game is fucking stupid. Although he logically knew it, he didn't open his mouth to correct the assumption that Zoey was a date. He enjoyed seeing the fire in her eyes. *I'm such an asshole.*

When he handed Morgan back the file, she nodded to him and turned to Zoey with a smile. "It was nice meeting you. Sorry about interrupting your . . . lunch."

Morgan had impressed him. She could do the job. But that didn't stop him from watching the sway of her hips as she turned and left the office. I *like the fire in you. And technically, you're not my employee so you wouldn't be breaking any HR policies if we hooked up.*

Before he could think further of the things he'd like to do with her, Zoey reminded him she was still there, waiting.

"Oh, dear brother. With that look on your face, you're definitely having lunch with me."

"I'd love to, but running two companies doesn't really leave time for playing twenty questions with you over a long lunch."

Zoey stood up, but he knew better than to think she was defeated. *Hendersons don't give up. Unfortunately.*

"No problem. I'll go and see if the new employee has time for lunch so I don't have to eat alone."

Shaun rose from his seat, which Zoey knew he would. She had a way of tormenting her brothers until she got her way. If she ever decided to use it in business, she'd be the scariest of them all. Her tactics, although subtle, were extremely effective.

"One hour, Zoey. Your choice, eat or talk, but you've got only one hour, understood?"

She linked her arm in his and laughed softly. "I think I'll eat, and you can talk. The conversation is going to be so much more interesting that way."

And again I ask myself: why the hell did I say yes to

Dean?

As he sat across from Zoey, his mind strayed back to Morgan. There was something about her, but he couldn't put his finger on it.

"Okay, Shaun, you might as well tell me what's troubling you."

Normally he'd keep his concerns to himself, but not after the year they'd just had. He downed the last of his coffee before speaking.

"I can't stop thinking about Morgan."

Zoey nodded. "Ah, the new employee. I was hoping you'd bring her up."

He raised a hand to stop where her thoughts were going. "It's not what you think."

"And what do I think?" Zoey had a grin on her face as she knew she'd cornered him.

He wasn't going to take the bait. "We never saw it coming last time, the danger and betrayal, and all because someone came out of the shadows thinking we owed them something. I mean, Tim shooting Dean and kidnapping Tessa. That should be an eye opener to us all that we have targets on our backs. We can't just hire someone off the street."

Zoey sat quietly, watching him for minute. *Don't read more into this than what I said. I'm only concerned for the family. That's all.*

"And you think she's what exactly? A spy? A hitman? She seemed sweet and genuine to me."

Shaun shook his head. "No. But there is something

off about her. Did you know Dean hired her on the spot without speaking to her?"

"No. That is odd. But the way Dean goes through staff, what's the difference? If it weren't for Tessa, this place would probably close its doors because no one would work for him. God knows I couldn't."

Dean was tough to work for. He expected and demanded perfection. It made him successful when he didn't have people working beneath him. He was only a few years younger than Shaun, but he still had been able to make his mark in the business world. It was odd, because unlike him, Dean hadn't gone to college. He was more street-smart and was willing to take more risks. That could one day come with a high price. *Higher than getting shot.*

"He's not thinking this through. The only recommendation this woman had was from Lexi Chambers."

Zoey laughed and almost choked on her coffee. "That would be a red flag for me. I mean she's nice and everything, but reliability isn't her strength."

"I can't understand why Dean kept her on as long as he did."

"Oh, that's simple. Tessa likes her, and she really did a great job. I can't believe she up and quit like that, but that's Lexi. So what are you going to do about Morgan? I can see it's driving you crazy."

He knew what he'd do if it were his company. *Actually I never would have hired her, so I guess I wouldn't have this issue.*

"I need to find out about her background."

"You mean to get her references?"

"Those can be falsified easily."

"Well, I still have Bennett Stone's number if you want it. Really think it through before going down that path. If you're interested in her in any way, I would suggest asking her and not investigating her."

I'm not interested. He could tell himself that over and over again, but his body told a different story. It didn't change that he needed to find out how she managed to show up at Poly-Shyn at the perfect time. Shaun didn't believe in coincidences or fate. There was more to the story, and he was going to find out what it was. If things didn't add up, he wanted her out of there before Tessa and Dean returned. The last thing anyone needed was another incident.

"Just give me the number and don't worry about how I obtain the answers. Just know that I will." *We can't afford to be blindsided like that again. If Dean isn't on top of his game, then I'll have to watch his back for him.*

Chapter Three

MORGAN COULDN'T GET home fast enough. She didn't know why seeing Shaun Henderson with another woman bothered her, but it had. The rest of the day, no matter how she tried to concentrate on her work, the words on the screen became one big jumble. No matter what she tried, she thought of him. It was maddening and not like her.

It had been years since she'd held a high-level position in a company, but that had been her choice. There were things in her life that meant more than making the big money. Her old company, WS & Son, always told her it was a one-time special circumstance, but she often ended up traveling for extended periods of time. Once she'd not only went overseas, she had also negotiated a better deal than her counterpart. That's when she learned it was possible to do too good of a job. *They dumped it all on me, but the ones who weren't pulling their weight kept their jobs at the same pay and got to coast by while I worked my ass off. Nope. Never again.*

Of course her prior experience hadn't been at a company nearly as prestigious as Poly-Shyn, but she had always prided herself in giving one hundred percent to her job. She couldn't say that was the case today, and she was disappointed in herself. She might be doing something she'd never done before, but she expected more from herself than acting like a daydreaming teenager.

He was nothing to her but a distraction. *Actually, for a week he's my boss, but besides that he's nothing.*

She'd have to give him credit for his great taste in women though. As soon as she entered Shaun's office, his date's smile and beauty filled the room. The woman dressed for power, and her olive skin, high cheekbones, chestnut hair, and honey brown eyes were to die for. Morgan would like to think the woman had a bitch of a personality, but her intuition said otherwise. *I couldn't compete with that even if I tried.*

What was she thinking? She was not interested in Shaun. She'd played the dating game long ago and found life could be cruel. She wasn't about to let thoughts of such things enter her mind. Love wasn't ever going to be a reality for her. *Especially with someone like Shaun. He'd never understand. Never accept. People like him love money above all else.*

She pulled her purse from her desk drawer, ready to head home. It had been a long day, and this was only day two; it wasn't going to get any better until Dean was back. *At least, I'm not attracted to him.*

She had to face the fact she found him not just attractive, but damn, that man was sexy. It didn't help the way he looked at her. Was it her imagination or just wishful thinking, that he was undressing her with his eyes? *Does it matter? Nothing is going to happen. I saw the type of woman he likes. I'm not that woman any longer. I'm a T-shirt and blue jeans type now, and she was a designer diva all the way. People like that belong together.*

She spent her ride home trying not to think of him. It was easier said than done. Thankfully once inside she had other things to keep her mind preoccupied and the evening flew by.

Morgan flipped off her television, unable to remember what the news had been about. She got off the couch and headed to the bedroom. Cracking the door open slightly she peeked in to check on her son, Tyler. He was fast asleep. Morgan blew him a kiss from the door. *Sweet dreams angel. Mama loves you.*

As she closed the door and walked into her own bedroom she knew this was her reality. It was just her and Tyler. His father, Walter Sapp Jr., didn't want anything to do with him once he found out Tyler was autistic. "There's no reason why we can't be happy. All you need to do is give him up for adoption, and we can still be together." Walter had said that when Tyler was three. Morgan's only response to him was a hard slap across his face. He'd walked out of their lives that day and never contacted them again—emotionally or financially. As far as Morgan was concerned, they were better off without him and his judgmental family. In a blink of an eye, half of Tyler's family disappeared from his life.

Morgan had spent weeks crying over it at first. She'd left him messages, texts, and letters with pamphlets explaining autism, but nothing changed. One day she just stopped trying. *I can't make anyone love or accept him. They need to want to do it on their own. And people like Walter and his family will never change. As far as they're concerned we're damaged goods, not good enough for them. What they don't get, is they're not good enough for us.*

There was only one thing Tyler needed in his life: unconditional love. Morgan had that in abundance. But she wasn't going to cut Walter any slack. There was no excuse he could ever give to explain his actions. *Six years and not one word. You have no idea what you've given up. What you've missed. Your son is amazing. And you're nothing but a selfish ignorant fool. You don't deserve to be his father, and I'll never allow you to hurt him again. Never.*

Lying on her bed, she pulled the blanket up and closed her eyes. Tyler was everything to her. There was nothing and no one more important. She walked away from the job at WS & Son because she couldn't work for Tyler's grandfather, Walter's dad, any longer. Staff meetings became cold and awkward. She couldn't walk down a hallway without hearing whispers. What they were saying didn't matter. She was done. When she told her parents she was thinking of quitting, they fully supported her decision. Like Walter did to her and Tyler, the day she walked out she never looked back. No one called to question why. Morgan was sure one of the many people that had been nipping at her heels, waiting for her position as contract manager in purchasing, slid right into the job. That company was filled with people who drove hard for success and didn't care who they stepped on to get it. They had one love in life, and that was money. There was no room in her life for people like that.

Over the years she'd surrounded herself with friends who understood and accepted them as they were. *We are so much more than just a single mother and a young child with a disability. If you can't see that, then you don't belong in our lives.*

It had been years since she'd felt lonely in her bed, but tonight she was. No matter how she tried to deny it, her body was telling her otherwise. *Damn. Why him? Why not some nice simple man who wouldn't break our hearts? Because that's exactly what Shaun would do if given the chance.*

If it were just her, maybe she'd risk it all for a fleeting romance. But Tyler didn't have a father in his life and certainly didn't need strange men coming in and out of it. No. She might be lonely tonight, but it would pass. *It has to.*

"WHAT EXACTLY ARE you worried about?" Bennett asked.

Shaun leaned forward on his elbows on the desk. "You of all people should recall what happened with Tim."

Bennett nodded. "I do. Has your brother recently fired anyone new to cause you concern for a backlash?"

Who the hell knows what Dean does? He doesn't share anything with us. Hell, none of us share. Shaun couldn't remember the last time he discussed anything business never mind personal with his siblings. *Oh Dad, you really left your mark on this family and not in a good way.*

"There's just something off. I can't put my finger on it. She showed up for a job dressed so casual you would think she was going to go for a walk in the park. Not a corporate position."

"That's also not a red flag. From everything you've told me about her so far, it sounds like she wasn't planning on being here. So tell me, Shaun, what is it about her that really is driving you nuts?" Bennett arched a brow.

What the hell kind of question was that? Shaun knew he'd been clear on what he wanted. All Bennett needed to do was investigate and provide the answers. He wasn't getting paid to question Shaun's motives.

"Are you saying you can't get the information I asked for?"

"I could have it in a matter of seconds, but that is not the point. Before I go digging into someone's life, I want to make sure the reason behind the intrusion is valid."

Shaun wasn't sure if it was valid or not. Actually, he didn't care. Right now he wanted to know everything there was to know about Morgan Pereira. "Bennett, I want everything you can find on her. Where she lives, where she came from, and mostly, how the hell did she end up here at Poly-Shyn. Got it?"

Bennett leaned back in his seat. "She's thirty-six, and until yesterday morning she worked at Sunrise Café. I understand her boss was a real piece of work, and Morgan stood up to him not just for herself but for the entire staff. Of course, the outcome was being fired on the spot, but trust me, the guy is a scumbag. She's better off not working there."

So what Lexi told Dean holds up. But there is more. I just know it. "What else?"

"Shaun, I told you she appears to be straight up who she says she is. But is this really about her, or is it about you?"

"How the hell can it be about me?" Anger filled him. Was Bennett trying to accuse him of not being able to be trusted? *If that's the case, buddy, you're going to need medical treatment when I get through with you. I would never fuck with my family. Nor will I let anyone else.*

"I saw her photo when I pulled her driver's license. She's . . . very attractive, wouldn't you say?"

Bennett had a sheepish grin on his face. And Shaun wanted to knock it off him. This had nothing to do with any attraction he might or might not have to her. *Yeah she's stunning. But I'm not a teenager ruled by my dick. I trust my gut. There's something. But what? That I don't know.* "This is strictly professional and about the security and wellbeing of my family."

Bennett didn't hold back his laughter, which only

pissed Shaun off even more. *Why the hell does my family continue to hire you?*

Bennett got up from his seat and said, "Shaun, think about what exactly it is that you want. When you have it figured out, call me. If you find anything suspicious, call me. If anything starts to go wrong, call me. But if it's her phone number you want, just ask her."

"You're a real asshole aren't you?" Shaun could feel the heat under his collar rising. He wasn't used to being spoken to so brazenly by anyone outside of the family. Even then it took everything within him to control his temper.

"To the core." Before he left, he turned back to Shaun and said, "Tell your sister I said hello."

Shaun knew Bennett had added that piece just to push him even further. *Or at least, that better be all there was to his little remark. You are not the man for my sister. She's been around assholes all her life. She doesn't need to date one too.*

Once alone he found himself thinking of Morgan all over again. He couldn't believe she'd been working in a coffee shop before slipping into the HR job. *Dean, you really are losing your mind if you think pouring coffee qualifies her to handle your payroll. It's your money, but come on brother, get your head out of your ass and think business.*

Dean had been as cutthroat as they come. He was right up there with Asher Barrington, Trent Davis, and Dax Marshall. If he didn't pull himself out of whatever he was going through, he would lose his edge for good.

Until you get back from Paris, Dean, I'll make it look like you're on your game, but after that, it's all on you.

Shaun got up and slipped on his suit coat. Then he picked up his cell phone and slid it into the breast pocket. Tonight hadn't given him what he'd wanted, but that wasn't about to stop him. Tomorrow was another day, and he would do the digging into Morgan's past himself. *How hard can it be to make her divulge her little secrets to me? I bet with one kiss I could have her giving me the pin number to her bank card if I wanted it.*

Chapter Four

MORGAN HAD MANAGED to make it through the entire day without once bumping into Shaun. It took a lot more effort on her part than she wished, but the result was what she wanted. *A day without seeing his handsome face.*

That didn't mean she didn't think of him throughout the day. Each time her phone rang she secretly hoped it would be him asking her to come to his office. Once there he'd tell her he'd been thinking of her all day, pull her into his embrace, and kiss her until she forgot her name.

Morgan felt her cheeks warm. *Easy girl. This is a man I swore I wanted nothing to do with. So why the heck am I fantasizing about his lips and running my hands down his rock-hard abs? I don't even know if he has abs. For all I know he wears a man girdle and has a huge beer belly.*

Her laughter filled the small office and seemed to echo down the hall. *I wish he were butt ugly. Maybe then I wouldn't feel the need to stand in front of the air conditioner all the time.* Still laughing, she closed her eyes and fanned herself with a sheet of paper to cool the blush on her cheeks.

"I'm glad you're enjoying your new job. Would you care to share what you find so amusing?" Shaun asked, appearing out of nowhere.

Really? How does he keep sneaking up on me? His body filled the doorway. She knew he was tall, but seeing him in the doorframe showed how broad his shoulders were as well. *Stop looking at him. It's only going to make it worse.* Her pulse quickened as he stared at her. *Darn, you, Shaun. Another few minutes and I would've made it out of here.*

"Do you need something, Mr. Henderson?" Morgan asked, the laugh and smile no longer existing.

"No. I haven't seen you so I thought I'd check to make sure everything was okay. No issues."

Her first two days had been filled with such scrutiny she flinched each time she heard his name. He was casual and calm with her today, and it threw her off. Her mind instantly went through the list Lexi had given her. Had she missed something? *Or could I have done something incorrectly? People's lives could be affected if payroll hadn't run properly. What the heck was I thinking, taking a job so critical to the employees?*

"Is everything okay? You seem . . . nervous."

He didn't move from where he stood, so there was no way she could make a hasty getaway even if she had a viable excuse to leave.

She'd mentally made it through the checklist. Nothing came to mind that would've brought the boss down to her tiny office.

"I have no issues. Was there something specific you are inquiring about?"

He nodded and finally left the doorway and came to sit on the corner of her desk. *Don't you want the seat across from me? Farther away from me?*

"Why are you here?"

The question was too general. How was she to answer him? Did he mean in her office, in this building, in Boston? Shaun didn't appear to be the type to ask something just for small talk, so what exactly was his agenda?

"Because I work here." She knew that wasn't the answer he was looking for, but ask vague and receive vaguer. If there was something more he needed, he better speak quickly because the clock was ticking, and it was just about quitting time. Although she was enjoying her role in HR, she still had to get home for Tyler. It was important to keep to a strict routine. Any variation upset him, and she avoided that at all costs. *Dinner at six, then homework, shower, and bed by eight thirty.*

Morgan looked at the clock on the wall. It was already five past five. *Darn. I better get out of here quick, or it's not going to be a good night for us.*

"I was looking for more."

She met his eyes and thought for sure she'd see sarcasm, but there wasn't any. Did he really want to talk to her? And if so why now? What changed?

"Sorry Mr. Hen—"

"Shaun."

I know your name. It haunted my dreams last night. But I don't want to get that comfortable with you. The last thing I need is to be more attracted to you than I already am. Morgan could challenge him by continuing to call him Mr. Henderson, but if she did she would never be home in time for Tyler. Answer the question and get out. He was there for a purpose; she just needed to figure out what exactly that was.

"Shaun, I'm sorry, but I don't understand what you're asking. There haven't been any issues that weren't handled in the allotted time frame. Was there something I've overlooked that I could address tomorrow?"

Morgan was sincere. She might not understand all the ins and outs of HR, but she wanted to perform her duties correctly. *I'm getting paid to do a job. I expect to do it right.*

All her life she'd been so critical of herself. Her parents always told her they didn't expect perfection from her. But she did. If she said she'd do something, she wouldn't stop until it was done better than anyone had expected. *Whatever I'm lacking on this job, I'll figure it out and fix it right away. I just need to know what it is.*

"Nothing has been brought to my attention."

"Then why are you here?"

He laughed softly. "That was my original question."

And back to square one. This can go on for hours, and time is not something I have right now. She really didn't want to break the civil moment they were sharing, but it couldn't be avoided.

"Shaun, not that I'm not enjoying this conversation, but I need to be somewhere and have to leave now, or I'll be late. Can we pick up where we left off tomorrow?" *Since we're talking in circles, it won't be too hard.*

"A date?" His brow arched and his tone changed slightly.

Oh, wouldn't that be nice? But in reality, I do have a date with the most amazing young man, and I'm about to miss it. Her personal life was just that. She wasn't about to share it with him or anyone else at Poly-Shyn. It would only open her up to the same criticism she'd faced all those years ago. No understanding why someone with her potential didn't want to climb the cooperate ladder, why she would throw away a successful career, and for what? *The best thing that ever happened to me. Being a mother. It's a very hard job, but he is so worth it; he's such a loving boy. Coworkers can't understand this choice. Shaun comes from exactly what I left behind, and that's where it needs to stay. In the past.*

"Would you like to schedule time with me tomorrow? I can check my calendar to see what I have open." Morgan opened her laptop again and was about to sign in when Shaun reached out and closed it.

Her eyes flew up and met his gaze. They were dark and piercing. Had she upset him by ignoring his inappropriate question? If so that was his issue, not hers. She worked in HR, and it was her responsibility to maintain professionalism, and that included any form of sexual harassment. *Is it harassment if I want him? Probably not. Oh God. What if I'm the one doing the harassing? Could he be picking up on my little lustful thoughts? Could I be making him feel uncomfortable?*

The answer was clear as he bent toward her and kissed her gently on the lips. *Oh shit! I can't do this.* But she didn't pull away. Instead, she found herself leaning into him. That was all the encouragement she needed to give him, and his lips took hers eagerly. His hand reached out to cup the side of her face, drawing her even closer.

Morgan moaned as his tongue traced her lips, begging her to open to him. Any strength to resist was overshadowed by the raw need within her. She wanted his kisses, to feel his touch, to feel alive as a woman again. She'd been alone since . . .

No. I can't do this. I promised myself. It's only going to end badly, and I can't go through that again. It was painful, but she forced herself to put a hand on his chest and gently push him away. His hold on her tightened, then suddenly he released her. The absence of his touch and lips left her feeling empty and filled with yearning. *Oh shit, it's already too late; I want this man.*

He didn't try to stop her as she opened the bottom drawer of her desk, pulled out her purse, and left him sitting on her desk. She was too flustered to speak to him. *This wasn't supposed to happen. It shouldn't have happened. How am I going to face him tomorrow and then the next day?* All the way home she lectured herself on keeping her distance. *Nothing like giving the man mixed signals. Moan with sheer pleasure as he kisses me and then push him away and say nothing when I walk out. If he didn't have any concerns about me before, I'm sure he's got them now.*

When she arrived home her mother was just putting the plates on the table.

"I was beginning to worry you were working late and would miss dinner."

Morgan kissed her mother's cheek. "Mom you don't know how much I appreciate you staying a bit later tonight. I was worried I was going to need to make a peanut butter and jelly sandwich for Tyler."

"Tyler wouldn't ever complain about that. Sit down for a minute. You look like you've had a tough day. Want to talk about it?"

No way. But I know better than say nothing. Nothing is an admission of guilt. "Starting a new job is always tough, Mom."

Her mother, Elisabeth, sat down and patted the chair next to her. "Come on dear. Tell me all about it."

Morgan forced a smile and caved in, taking the seat offered. "I am out of my comfort zone; that's all."

"Morgan, you're brilliant. I've never seen you take on a challenge and not exceed everyone's expectations. So why is this any different?" Elisabeth reached out and covered Morgan's hands, which had been clamped together nervously on the table.

She was very close with her mother. They were beyond family, and over the last several years their relationship had grown to best friends. *If you can't share this with a friend, then who can you share it with?*

"Would kissing the owner's brother on my third day of employment be considered being an overachiever?" Morgan shook her head as she spoke. Even saying it, the words sounded ludicrous. Not the type of behavior anyone would expect from her.

Elisabeth's eyes widened, and her mouth gaped open before she burst out laughing. "Well, I guess your day wasn't boring after all. Since you opened the door, spill the details about how you managed to kiss one of the most eligible bachelors in Boston."

How do you know this, Mom? Oh yeah, you follow the gossip columns. You don't miss much do you? That didn't mean she was going to tell her mother that Shaun had a girlfriend. Kissing a man who was attached, even if he was just dating, was a shame she was going to have to bear. *Of course, it's a shame that should be shared. How could you even think about kissing me? And how could I kiss you back? Damn, this is going to get complicated. We cannot ever let it happen again. I'll make that perfectly clear tomorrow.*

Tyler walked into the room like clockwork. He didn't say a word, just sat in his seat, waiting for dinner.

Thank you, Tyler, for saving Mommy from a very awkward explanation. "Looks like we will have to finish this another time, Mom."

Morgan got up and kissed her son on the top of his head. *I've missed you, my precious boy.*

Tyler pointed to the dish of spaghetti and meatballs in the center of the table.

"Use your words, Tyler."

It was a reminder that she may need to give him for the rest of his life, but every time he spoke the words touched Morgan's heart.

"Mommy, I'm hungry. Time to eat."

"Yes, Tyler. Time to eat."

She kissed him again on the head before serving his food. He looked up at her and smiled. *Love you, Tyler.*

Whatever her day was like, good or bad, coming home to her son made it a perfect night. *This is what my life is. And it's a great life. Remember that. Life is not a romance novel. It's not happily ever after.*

SHAUN RESISTED THE urge to grab her wrist and pull her back into his arms. When he went down to her office, it wasn't with the intention of kissing her. It was to gather information Bennett was reluctant to get for him. *Tasting her sweet lips hadn't been on my list, but damn it should've been.*

Watching the sway of her hips as she scurried down the hall to escape him didn't help to cool him off any. She may have stopped the kiss, but it wasn't because she wasn't enjoying it. He felt her passion, her desire for him. It was something else that made her pull away so abruptly. *Maybe she has a boyfriend. Or she's married.*

He ran his hand through his hair and stood up. Answers weren't going to come to him. He needed to go get them. If Bennett wasn't willing to help, then he was going to take the initiative to seek them out himself.

He pulled out his cell phone and called for the limo. He wasn't sure where to start, but he'd never given up on anything he wanted before. Right now he wanted to know everything there was to know about Morgan.

While waiting for the car to arrive, his phone rang. Dean. The call didn't come as any surprise, as the family still kept him at a distance when it came to business affairs. *Maybe someday they'll understand.*

Shaun tried to assist his family with financial advice, but they never wanted to hear it. He understood why. They all felt the wrath of their father, but Shaun had mastered the art of persuasion at a young age. It didn't mean his father loved him or even respected him, but it meant he'd been able to talk his way out of things a bit better than the rest of his siblings. In that household, that was enough to raise a red flag.

He didn't blame them for not trusting him. Most people thought he was kissing his father's ass. The truth was all these years he knew to keep his enemies close. And his enemy was his father, James Henderson. So he had worked closely with their father at Poly-Shyn. Not because he loved the man, and surely not because their father had any love or respect for Shaun. Someone had to keep a close eye on him. Over the years, Shaun had caught wind of their father's manipulating ways to

continue to hurt the family. It hadn't been easy, sometimes taking the hit himself, but he'd always been able to
put a stop to it. They might not ever know what he'd
done, or even believed it, but he had the emotional scars
to prove it. *And you checking up on me, Dean, is proof this
family still doesn't trust me. And probably never will.*

"Hope you're not calling to talk about flowers or
dresses because I'll disconnect the call quickly."

Dean laughed. "You have no idea what this trip is
like. I'd rather be thrown into the lions' pit and need to
negotiate my way out. Really, how many shades of
purple can there be?"

"I'll pass on that."

"For now, Shaun. Someday this will be you." Dean
laughed again.

I can guarantee that will never be me. He wasn't about
to get back on the topic of a few days ago. Why the
family all of a sudden thought he needed someone in his
life was beyond him. If they wanted to play matchmaker,
they could do it with Logan or Alex. His sister, on the
other hand . . . he wasn't sure there ever would be
anyone good enough for her. *Actually, I know there won't
be.*

"Was there something else you wanted to talk
about?"

"Yes. I received the contact for the deal in Florida."

Shaun knew exactly which one that was. He'd reviewed it and given it back to Donald himself the first
day. "Good, I told Brittany-Lynn to make sure to send it

once it was typed up for final signature."

"Yeah. The changes you made were right on. Good call, Shaun. Thanks."

Changes? I didn't approve any changes. If I didn't then who the hell did? Shaun had no idea what Dean was talking about. That document was prepared exactly as Dean had instructed. Since Dean was pleased, mentioning that tidbit of information didn't seem important. *It doesn't matter that you liked them; I'm more worried that someone broke protocol and made changes to what should've been a final document. Are they testing the waters to see if it would go unnoticed until they make their move on something much bigger? That is something Dad would've done. It's impossible to be him, so who then?* Digging into who made the changes was going to be a top priority in the morning. Things like this sometimes take time and manpower. He had both. This wasn't going to be overlooked. *Not while I'm around.*

"Once I have your signed copy I'll get it submitted for processing."

"Next time you make a change, make a note on it. It was just luck that I caught this one."

Open your damn eyes, Dean. Get your head back in business where it needs to be. But until you do, I've got this. Going forward he was going to need all contracts sent to him first, and he would forward them to Brittany-Lynn. Dean finally had turned Poly-Shyn around. A huge screw-up on a contract could tank everything Dean had done to bring Poly-Shyn back on top, and that made them a target.

"You've got it."

Shaun entered the limo, and instead of looking into Morgan's past tonight as he had expected to, he needed to do some different digging.

He called Bennett. He might not want to assist with Morgan, but he knew he'd work with a mystery. Whoever was messing with the contracts needed to be stopped before any damage was done.

"What do you need now, Shaun?"

"Hope you're still local, because I need you back at Poly-Shyn."

"Not more girl problems, I hope," Bennett teased.

Shaun was not in the mood for any of his shit today. *Can't this man just take a fucking order and do it? How did he make it all those years in the Marines with smart ass remarks?*

Shaun was tempted to see who else could be pulled in, but Bennett was very familiar with the history of Poly-Shyn and probably still had all the background checks on the employees. He was the logical choice.

Bennett told Shaun to email him a copy of the contract that had been changed, and he would start digging into it.

"I've kept my ears close to the ground for the past several months, Shaun. Whatever is going on doesn't seem to intend harm to the company. Give me until sometime next week, and I'll let you know what I find.

So much for having a turnaround time of a few seconds.

"I was hoping to have an answer before Dean and Tessa return."

"If I thought there was even the slightest risk, I'd have my men there now."

Shaun had no choice but to trust Bennett's expertise. Not only did he come highly recommended by their brother Brice, but he'd saved Tessa's and Dean's lives. *Got to cut a man like that some slack. But he better have some answers next week.*

"If you're wrong—"

"I'm not."

He disconnected the call. Shaun liked to be in control so he could predict the outcome. Having to rely on another person was foreign to him. That didn't mean he wasn't going to do some digging himself while waiting.

Morgan, you're going to have to wait. But trust me, I won't forget about you.

Chapter Five

"ZOEY, I'M TELLING you, something is going on. I can't put my finger on it."

"Shaun, we all still look over our shoulders thinking we see a shadow approaching. But we can't live our lives like that forever."

He knew she wanted to get back to a normal life. That was why he was so diligent in keeping an eye open. He'd failed to see the threat Tim was. He'd dropped the ball, thinking things had changed, but the reality was there would always be haters lurking, maybe not violent ones, but they were there. That was why all these years he'd stayed so close to Poly-Shyn. But when needed most, he'd shut himself off. He told himself it was because he was so busy with work, but that wasn't the truth. He really thought once their father had died no one else could hurt them to the extent he had. *How wrong I was. I'll never make that mistake again.*

"If it means protecting the family, then that's what we need to do. Don't trust anyone."

He could see she hated hearing those words. Their

childhood had been horrendous, and now he was telling her their adult life wasn't going to be any happier. *Hate me if you must. As long as you're safe, I don't care.*

"That's easy for you to say, Shaun. You like keeping your distance from everyone. But some of us are tired of living that way. Look at Brice and Dean. If they can find happiness out of all the craziness we grew up with, then why not me? Why not you?"

Because I spent too many years working close with Dad, trying to read him, understand him, get into his psyche so far that I'm not sure I can get him out of mine. No one deserves to be exposed to that level of madness. It should've died with him, but I feel as though he's infected me with his bitterness and hate.

"Zoey, you'll find someone someday." *He'll just have to pass my interrogation first.*

She slumped into the couch in the office. "I don't know. Lately, I don't have an inclination to date. Well, there is one, but I don't think he's interested."

Shaun raised a brow. Zoey had never spoken of a man before. At least, not in a very long time. If there was someone coming around now, he needed to know. "Who is it? What's his name? How did you meet?"

She let out a long sigh. "Let's see how to put it. Oh yeah, none of your business. I'm your *big* sister, remember? My job to take care of you. Not the other way around."

Enjoy it. But I'll find out. I have resources. Just another thing to put on Bennett's list. "Okay, so we have an understanding. You stop asking about Morgan, and I'll stay out of your personal life."

The grin on her face wasn't convincing. She was up to something. If he weren't so concerned about who was playing with the Poly-Shyn contracts, he'd push the subject with her even further.

"So what are you planning on doing? Dean is coming back Monday. There is no reason for you to stay on. You can go back to your office, run your own business."

"I spoke to Dean briefly earlier this morning. He doesn't believe there's an issue, but he agreed an added pair of eyes here for the short-term would be beneficial. The vacant office next to Dean's will be set up this weekend. I'll be working from there until further notice."

Her eyes widened with disbelief then softened to her usual happy self. "Good. That means when I show up for my unexpected lunch dates, I can drag you along with Dean. I wonder how many other brothers I can get to move their offices here?" She was tapping her chin as though her mind was already plotting.

"I'm not here to play, Zoey," he said in a firm voice, but she ignored him as expected.

"Not Logan as he needs to stay close to the hospital. But Alex could and probably should move here. Have you seen his office? It looks like something from a sci-fi movie. There's nothing inviting about it. I told him he needs a leather couch so when he gets bored he can take a nap. You'd think he could've found some humor in that, but for once, he didn't crack a smile." She looked off into the distance in deep thought. "I think I'd better go and check on him when I'm done with you."

Please go now. I'm sure he needs your "help" more than I do. "Good, tell him I said hello."

She gave him a look saying she didn't appreciate him kicking her out of the office. "You're lucky I want to miss the Friday night rush-hour traffic. I'm surprised you haven't already left. Are you hanging around in hopes of seeing Morgan again?"

He shot her a warning look. She raised her hands in surrender, but her laughter said she'd won.

"Good night, Zoey. Now go home and remember what I said. Keep your eyes open."

She nodded and walked over to where he sat; leaning forward she gave him a huge hug. *What the heck? I don't do hugs. You know that. Is there something you're not telling me, Zoey?* When he looked into her eyes, he saw a hint of sadness he'd not seen before. Had it been there all along, and he was too damned absorbed in his own shit to notice?

"Zoey, is everything okay?" His voice was clearly filled with concern. But he didn't care. This was his sister and what affected her, affected him.

"Tired I guess; I haven't been sleeping very well lately."

"Why?"

"I've been getting these headaches. Must be stress. You're right. It's time to go home."

When she let go of him, he grabbed her hand and

asked, "Do you want me to drive you?"

Zoey laughed, but he could tell it was forced. "You're not going to cramp my style by hovering over me on a Friday night. Good try."

Shaun waited until she left his office then picked up the phone and dialed his brother Logan.

"What's up Shaun?"

"Do me a favor. Stop in and check on Zoey this weekend. Don't tell her I asked."

There was a slight pause then Logan asked, "Shaun, what's going on? You don't sound yourself at all."

"Just do it, Logan. It might be nothing, but just do it."

"Will do."

He hung up the phone but now was more stressed than before. *Keep an eye on Poly-Shyn, and an eye on Zoey and the rest of the family, and which eye is supposed to watch Morgan? I guess I'll have to work on her on the weekends. Like this weekend.*

He buzzed Brittany-Lynn. "Get me Morgan's home address."

"Yes, sir."

I don't need Bennett to do this. I'm a great judge of character. All I'll need to do is see her five minutes in her own environment, and I'll have my answer.

MORGAN HAD EXPECTED to hear from Shaun first thing in the morning but she didn't. Maybe he was regretting yesterday as much as she was. *Honestly, I regret my reaction to the kiss more than the kiss itself. Why did I have to enjoy it so much? Couldn't it have sucked just a little? No. Instead, it had to be the most amazing kiss I've ever had. It was both giving and taking at the same time. If this is what a simple kiss is like with him, I wonder what it would be like to . . . Oh, don't even think about it. It was bad, dreaming last night of his lips tracing down my neck, over my collarbone, down my—.*

There was a knock on her office door. It was Donald whom she had stopped and talked to yesterday morning. Nice young man who, like everyone else in the company, was trying to climb the corporate ladder. One of his files had been sent to her office in error and curiosity led from one thing to another. *Hence, why he's here now.*

"Sorry to bother you, but I wanted to thank you for yesterday. That suggestion was perfect. I don't know why I never thought about including it."

Morgan smiled. "It was my pleasure." *Truthfully, it felt good reviewing a contract again even if I wasn't the one to negotiate the terms. If I can help even in a small way, then I will.*

"Do you have a few minutes to take a look at another one that I'm working on now?" He looked hesitant about asking. She understood why. In this cut-throat business world, the more information she had, the more likely she'd be able to take over doing his job, and he'd find himself unemployed. What no one knew was she'd managed a team of people doing exactly what Donald does. Even then, they were all young and eager to learn, and all itching to take her job. *They can have it. That's not my life any more.*

"Please come in and take a seat. Let's see what you've got."

He did as she asked and handed her the multi-page document. It was clear the kid had potential and one day would be a strong asset to this company. All he needed was some guidance. In this business knowledge was power. Morgan lived with the belief that knowledge not shared was a waste.

As she reviewed it, there were a few concerns that jumped out at her. When she pointed them out to him and told him the options for either rewording it or excluding it, he seemed to grasp the logic behind the changes.

"I really don't know how you know all this stuff, Morgan, but Poly-Shyn could use you in contracts. We are all used to submitting it, and Dean kicking it back filled with red lines for edits. Yesterday was the first time a contract came back clean."

Wow. Guess I've still got it. "As I said yesterday, I'm happy to help you, Donald, but this is our little secret. I'm in HR, not contracts."

"I don't feel right about taking credit for your ideas. Maybe if Dean knew what you're capable of, he'd consider using you."

Using me. Yep. That sounds about right. I'm tired of being used. All I want to do is come in, do my job, and go home. I'm not out to impress Dean or anyone else. Not anymore.

"If you want my help, this stays between us." She used her management warning tone. One that says last chance. He seemed to pick up on it as well.

"It's your loss. You're not going anywhere in HR, but move to contracts and you get to see the entire business picture. You'd be amazed how quickly you can get promoted."

Not surprised at all. But the higher you climb, the harder you fall. As he left her office she called out to him, "Donald, good luck with your document."

He waved and nodded as he quickly left. No matter how much he told her he wanted Dean to know she was the one behind the changes, she knew he didn't. If so he would've shared her skill with others in the contract department, and she'd have a line at her door. *Better this way. The fewer people who know, the better. I already get questioning looks from Shaun. I don't need Dean inquiring too deeply. I've got the job, so everyone should just leave me alone to do it.*

Helping Donald only set her back a half hour. It was nothing she couldn't make up Monday morning. With no one looking over her shoulder, things were finished quickly. The only problem was if she had a question, there wasn't anyone to ask for help. Lexi told her Tessa was wonderful to work for. *I guess I'll find out next week when she returns. It will be a nice change to work for a laid-back person. A real nice change.*

Morgan had to admit that her first week of work

went so much better than she'd expected. If it hadn't been for Shaun, she'd actually say it had been perfect. There was only an hour left on a Friday afternoon. It was time to slow down, coast a bit.

There were files that she'd requested earlier. She picked up the phone to call someone in the file room to come and retrieve them but didn't dial the number. *I've been sitting too long. So not used to this. If I don't keep moving, I'm going to gain a hundred pounds.*

Picking up the files, she decided to deliver them herself. When the elevator doors opened, she immediately realized it was going to be one uncomfortable ride down to the ground floor. She nodded as she entered, then faced the doors, not wanting to make eye contact. Morgan was riddled with guilt over the kiss. *This is ridiculous. It was nothing.*

"I don't know if you remember me from Shaun's office earlier this week."

Oh, I do. You're his stunningly perfect girlfriend. "Yes, I do. How are you?" It was painful to look at her, knowing he probably kissed her that night and went home to this woman.

She reached out a hand and said, "I'm Zoey Henderson."

Morgan thought she'd faint. *His wife. Oh, my God. I should've known someone like him wasn't single. If I'd known, I never would've . . . I shouldn't have anyway. What type of person am I? What type of person is he?*

Her hand trembled as she shook Zoey's hand. "My

name is Morgan Pereira."

"That's a lovely name."

You're killing me. Don't be so darn nice to me. I'm a horrible person, and you should hate me as much as I hate myself right now. "Did you have lunch with your . . . husband again today?"

"Husband?" Zoey looked at her with a puzzled expression then the elevator filled with laughter. "Please don't tell me you thought Shaun and I were married." Zoey was holding her stomach from laughing so hard. "He's my kid brother."

Brother. Your brother. Relief and joy flooded through her. It took all her self-control not to jump for joy. *Easy. This really doesn't change anything. Nothing can happen between us. Our paths are too different. I'm all family, and he's all business.*

"I know it was only for a week, but how did you like working for him? He wasn't too tough on you was he?"

Tough? You wouldn't believe me if I told you. But no, I'm not sharing a thing. "Nothing I couldn't handle." Morgan smiled, thinking that gave the right impression. Zoey must know her brother was not an easy man to report to. Anything less than that response would bring suspicion. Besides, Dean was supposed to be back on Monday. She'd no longer need to deal with Shaun. *For business or pleasure.*

"I'm glad to hear it because I just left his office, and I get the impression he'll be hanging around a bit longer."

"Isn't Dean returning on Monday?" She hoped the

panic within her didn't come through in her voice.

"Yes he is, but Shaun, for some strange reason, asked Brittany-Lynn to set up an office next to Dean's. I have no idea what's going on. They are not partners, but whatever it is, Shaun said he wanted to stay close. Have you noticed anything unusual lately?"

Morgan shrugged. "I've only been here a week. It's all unusual to me. If you know anything more specific, I'd be happy to look into it."

"Oh, yeah. I forgot. Coming in from the outside and dealing with a Henderson is not easy. And this is coming from one. But if you can look past the surface, Morgan, you might like what you see."

The elevator doors opened, and they both got out on the ground floor. Before Zoey headed for the exit, she added, "Shaun comes across as hard and cold. But if you're even the slightest bit interested, then give him a chance to show you who he really is."

Interested? I never said anything. Why would she think I'm interested? Did Shaun tell her about the kiss? Oh, God. How embarrassing. And here I am covering HR, and I don't even follow the no fraternization policy myself. "There's nothing betw—"

"Save it for someone who believes it, Morgan. I'm a woman, and I know what I see. Besides, I know my brother, and it's not work that has him all tied in knots."

Morgan stood there, stunned. Zoey not only said it publicly but hadn't tried toning her voice to be discreet. She looked around and thankfully found the only other person in the lobby was the security guard. Although he was not looking at her, he had a grin on his face that said he heard. *There's nothing going on. I don't need my coworkers thinking there is.*

She didn't want to hang around to find out. It was bad enough as it was. Monday she was going to need to face Dean and Tessa. Had Zoey mentioned it to them? Was her new boss going to be giving her a lecture that she very well deserved? Either way, she was going to prepare herself for the worst and hope for the best.

At least, where the job is concerned. Shaun is a totally different matter. What Zoey said doesn't change anything. He knows nothing about me. Tyler and I won't fit in his perfect little world. Once his family finds out how we really live, their attitudes will change. I guarantee it.

Her intention was to stay a few minutes in the file room and get to know more of the staff. She was still so flustered after her brief conversation with Zoey that she wanted nothing more than to get back to the safe confines of her office and hide away until it was five o'clock. *This day can't end fast enough.* Without even meeting anyone's eyes, she dropped the files on an empty desk and hurried back to the elevator. She pretended not to notice the grin still on the guard's face. *Tomorrow I start looking for new employment.*

Chapter Six

S HAUN SAT OUTSIDE the two-family home. When Brittany-Lynn gave him Morgan's address he thought for sure it was an error. No one at the company lived outside of Boston in an area like this. But once there, he saw why someone would love it. It was a rural neighborhood. People were out jogging and walking their dogs. There was even a freestanding basketball hoop on the sidewalk so the kids could play from the road. That was something he never had the opportunity to do growing up. Playing wasn't allowed. *"It is a waste of time and will only make you weak."* *At least that's what good old dad told us every day.* There was a lot they missed doing. If there had been anyone playing, he might have been tempted to shoot a few too.

There were no neighborhood games where he grew up. They lived in a very affluent area where kids were not seen or heard. *It was all about appearances. Too bad no one ever realized what a fucked-up home we lived in. We had more money than God, but we might've been safer growing up on the streets. At least then there was a chance of not catching a beating, and someone might love us.*

No matter how bad it had been growing up, the one and only thing he was grateful for was his siblings. It wasn't a happy home, but they at least were together through the bad times. *Maybe it's time we find some good times to share.* He knew Brice and Dean had moved in that direction. He could see Zoey following their footsteps. Logan was so damn deep into his research with Jon Vinchi on whatever the next neurological surgical tool would be that he didn't think the man even took time to sleep, never mind date. That only left Alex, who took nothing seriously, not work or women.

Shaun never put himself into the equation. He dated frequently, but on a very casual/mutual understanding kind of way. *No future. No commitment.*

It didn't take long before people began to stare at the limo. It definitely wasn't an everyday occurrence. He should've thought of that earlier. Before he could have the driver pull away, a gray Honda Accord pulled into the driveway. A woman, who looked like an older version of Morgan, got out and walked to the back of the car and opened the trunk. He saw her trying to pick up a case of water.

Before he knew it, he was out of the limo and by her side. "Would you like some help with that?"

She turned and smiled at him as though she'd expected him. *How? We've never met before so why are you looking at me as though you know exactly who I am?*

"I would love it. Thank you. My husband usually

carries in all the heavy items, but he was called into work for a water main break across town. I have no idea when he'll be home."

And you're telling a perfect stranger that you are home alone? Not wise. I could be some lunatic and hurt you. As he carried the two cases of water toward the house, he saw the limo out of the corner of his eye. The driver was leaning against the car, watching him. *Yeah, he probably thinks I'm nuts right now too.*

She opened the door without even using a key and entered. *No lock. What the hell? Did I enter a parallel universe where crime and dysfunctional families don't exist?*

"The kitchen is straight ahead. If you could put them on the counter by the sink, that would be wonderful."

As he walked down the hall in the direction she pointed, he noticed the wall was covered with photos. He was getting to know them as each step brought him to more current ones. He quickly went to the kitchen, placed the water where she said, and headed right back to the hall. Something had caught his eye, and he wanted a closer look.

Morgan. She was there with a ballet costume on and looked like she was in grade school. *Cute.* Then another with her in a cheerleader outfit probably in high school. *Curvy even back then. Bet all the boys were chasing after her.* There was her high school grad picture with her parents, then one from college. He knew the building well. *Boston University. Nice. And surprising. I thought Bennett said she worked in a coffee house. Why?*

One more question on his growing list of things to ask her. As he came to the final row of pictures, Morgan was no longer alone. She held a baby, then a toddler, and finally a child who looked school age. *She has a child. A son.* He looked back through them and didn't see any male figure in the pictures with her.

"That's Morgan and her son, Tyler. He's a handsome young man isn't he?"

"Yes." He didn't turn from the picture. Her eyes were so full of life, of happiness. He could stand there all day looking at her. *And where is that smile when she's with me?* Maybe I haven't given her a reason to smile.

He thought back to the past week. He honestly didn't treat her worse than anyone else, but that didn't mean he treated her nicely either. *What can I say? I'm an asshole. I admit it.*

"Where's his father?" Shaun didn't even realize he voiced the question out loud, but he didn't regret doing so.

"He's a very . . . selfish person. He's not been in their life since Tyler turned three."

He turned from the picture and asked, "At all?"

She shook her head. "Morgan has done it all on her own. She's an amazing woman. When Walter, Tyler's father, walked out of their lives, she could've given up, but she didn't. Instead she worked even harder to give her son everything he needed and more."

What a fucking jerk. He has a son and a beautiful wife, and he abandoned them for what? Was it another woman?

The responsibility of being a father? Oh, I don't know him, but I would love to knock him on his weak, cowardly ass.

"Why don't you come and sit in the living room and have some lemonade while waiting for them to get back. She has a little apartment upstairs for her and Tyler, but they will stop here before going up. They always do."

Ah. She's not home. That explains why she hasn't burst in asking what the hell I'm doing here. "That would be nice."

"My name is Elisabeth, by the way."

"Shaun."

Once again there was that look in her eye that said, *I know.* Had Morgan talked about him? Judging how forthcoming Elisabeth was being, she must have. *Ah, so I wasn't just some stranger. But did she tell you what a jerk I've been? No. If she had, I probably wouldn't have even been allowed on the stoop, never mind sipping on lemonade in your home.*

As he sat listening to family stories of Morgan's youth, he knew he'd been so wrong about her. She was, as her mother said, amazing. He went to all the best schools, but she earned full scholarships and graduated with a 4.0. *Morgan, you are a mystery that I'm looking forward to getting to know better.*

As SHE ROUNDED the corner on the bicycle built for two, Tyler shouted, "Home Mommy. Home."

"Yes, Tyler. We're almost there." The house was just around the next bend, and he knew it. He loved to go for a ride, but she knew he couldn't be trusted to ride alone. He became easily distracted and had no concept of oncoming traffic. Never mind that he could wander away and easily get lost. So every weekend they went for a ride, which meant she did most of the pedaling, but she loved it. They both did, and it gave them an opportunity to get some fresh air, and her a little exercise. It had been a long winter, but they were going to enjoy spring to its fullest.

Before she saw the house, she noticed what was parked in the street in front of it. The limo looked as out of place as an elephant in a pet shop. There was a very slim chance it was Walter or his father. Neither of them would come to see her. And if they wanted to see Tyler, they wouldn't do it here. *A place below their class. Not that either of them have any.* That left only one person. *Shaun. What does he want that can't wait till I'm back at the office?* Morgan almost slammed on the brakes, but that would've startled Tyler. There was no choice but to keep going and pull into the driveway. *I don't know what he's doing here, but whatever it is, please don't do it in front of my son.*

They parked the bike, and Tyler didn't even wait for her. He ran to the house, opened the door, and went in. Morgan saw a man leaning against the limo. She didn't follow Tyler. Instead, she went to confront him while they were alone.

"Where is he?" she asked the driver, who pointed to the house. Morgan was shocked at her abruptness, especially to someone who knew nothing of what was going on. She wanted to apologize, but that might require an explanation, which wasn't going to happen.

"He helped a woman carry in groceries about thirty minutes ago and hasn't come back out."

Shit. Not good. Not good at all. That meant Tyler was inside with Shaun. Whenever he was around someone new he became very nervous and started wildly shaking his hands in front of himself until he became comfortable. Sometimes he never calmed down, and they would need to leave. Unless her mother had told Shaun about Tyler, he would have no clue what was going on.

As she half ran toward the house, the memories of Walter flooded her mind. His hurtful words and how he'd treated Tyler. Even before they'd had the diagnosis, Walter laughed at their son's behavior. *If his own father could mock and laugh at him, what was Shaun going to do? Please don't laugh. He's just an innocent child who has feelings.*

Fear and anger filled her as she opened the door and began searching the house. Then she heard her mother say, "Tyler this is Mommy's friend, Shaun. Say hi to Shaun."

"Hi, Shaun," Tyler repeated.

Morgan stopped in her tracks, holding her breath, waiting to hear Shaun's reaction.

"Hello, Tyler," Shaun's voice echoed calmly from the living room.

Only then did she exhale and gain the courage to enter the room. Tyler was flapping his hands as expected.

Morgan turned to meet Shaun's eyes and prepared herself for the worst. She couldn't read his thoughts, but she saw that he was watching Tyler closely. *What are you thinking, Shaun?* His expression was serious, as though studying him, yet not like Walter or others had done. No matter what, she was uncomfortable with the entire situation. She had no time to prepare and her emotions were all over the place.

He only stopped looking at Tyler when Elisabeth made her presence known.

"How was your bike ride, Morgan?" Elisabeth asked.

"Great." She turned back to Shaun whose face was riddled with questions. Was he regretting coming here? *No one invited you. You can leave now. Nothing is stopping you. Make it quick. Just get it over with.* "Mom, I think Tyler might want a snack after that long ride. Would you mind taking him into the kitchen?" She wanted to make sure Tyler wasn't in earshot of whatever was going to be said between her and Shaun.

She saw the hesitation in her mother's eyes, but it was too late as Tyler heard the word snack and was already on the move to the kitchen.

"It was a pleasure meeting you, Shaun. I hope to see you again soon."

Don't count on it, Mom. He shouldn't be here now, never mind again.

"Thank you for the drink." Shaun handed her the empty glass before she left the room.

Once alone Morgan turned her full attention back to

Shaun. Still standing, now with her hands on her hips, she asked, "What are you doing here?"

Only then did he make eye contact with her. "Looking for you; there were a few questions I needed answers to."

I'm not buying it. Why are you really here? "Okay. What are they?"

She watched a grin appear. "Your mother answered them for me."

Oh, shit! Now I'm scared. What did you do, Mom? This is not the type of man you think he is. He's not here because he cares about me and Tyler. He's here because . . . hell I don't know why, but I know it's not good, whatever it is.

"And those questions were what exactly?"

He got up from the seat and walked over to her. "Don't worry. I have more than what I came for."

And that is what worries me. If you're not going to tell me, then I'll get it out of my mother. Obviously she has loose lips.

"Then I guess you can go now."

Shaun ignored her. "What's wrong with him?"

It felt like a punch in the gut or a hard slap in the face. She couldn't control her tone as she replied, "Nothing is *wrong* with him."

Apparently he knew she was hurt by his careless words; his tone became soft and defensive. "That's not what I meant. I only mea—"

"That he's odd? Different? Special?" she snapped at him accusingly.

"Don't put words in my mouth."

"I'm not. You're the one who implied it."

"Morgan."

He reached for her hand, but she pulled it away. She didn't want his touch or whatever lame excuse he was about to sputter out. She wanted nothing from him. It was obvious this was not what he expected when he arrived. *He probably is shocked to find I have a son, never mind one with special needs.*

"Morgan. Calm down. I don't understand why you're so upset."

Of course, you don't. You don't understand anything. Not what Tyler needs and not what I need. So stop trying to pretend you care.

"You're right. You don't. And you never will. Since you have your answers, Mr. Henderson, I think it's best you leave now." Her tone was dry, emotionless. She was not going to let him see how much this was truly hurting her. *Bury the feelings I have. If not for myself, then for Tyler's sake.*

He looked at her closely. "Is that what you truly want, Morgan?"

God no. I want you to pull me into your arms. Tell me that you find me amazing and my son super smart. That you want to take us to the zoo and spend the entire day getting to know us. Can't you see it? Are you blind or is it you don't want to see what is right there in front of you? We just want to belong, for someone to accept us as we are, flaws and all. I won't allow myself to say it, so you're going to have to figure it out yourself.

"Yes." It was short and simple but to the point. Yet she knew the word hurt her more than it did him.

He glared at her for a moment then said, "I'll see you in the office Monday," and walked out of the living room.

When she heard the front door close, she felt her body relax. That's when the tears started to flow. *Why? It's already difficult at work. Why come here and make it more difficult? What the hell does he want from me?*

Morgan shouted down the hall. "Mom, I'm going upstairs. I'll be back down for Tyler in a few."

Her mother came out of the kitchen just as the tears became a steady flow. Her voice filled with concern. "Morgan?"

"I can't right now, Mom." Morgan choked on her words. Elisabeth didn't say anything more, and Morgan ran up the stairway to her own apartment. She had to pull herself together before seeing Tyler. He would pick up on her emotions, and that wasn't fair to him.

Once inside she laid on her bed face down, blocking out the rest of the world. All the pain from Walter felt like it was just yesterday. Shaun coming here opened all the old wounds. Her reaction to him had nothing to do with him and everything to do with her.

She'd faced people before who judged or couldn't understand. Never had she treated them like this. Normally she pitied them for their ignorance. Something was different with Shaun. Everything was different. And it scared the hell out of her.

Damn you, Shaun. Damn you for making me want something more. I promised myself that I would never hope and dream again. Look at me now! Damn you. Morgan lifted her head from her pillow, wiped her cheeks, and sat on the edge of the bed. It was time to go downstairs and face her mother. She needed to explain Shaun's quick exit, and she needed to find out what the heck he was doing here in the first place. *I don't know why I even care. It doesn't matter. He's gone and won't be coming back.*

Chapter Seven

"MORGAN, YOU NEED to talk to him," Elisabeth said.

She sipped her morning coffee trying not to think of what she's going to be facing this morning. Weekends always went by too quickly; this one was no exception. The only difference is it wasn't the job that made her hate Monday. No matter how she cut it, it was inevitable that she was going to face one or more of the Hendersons today. *What have you told them, Shaun? Did you say I practically threw you out of my home?*

"I'm sure we will. I do work for them."

"You know that's not what I mean, Morgan. You haven't even talked about it. How do you expect to be able to go into work and not let it affect your performance?"

I have no idea. Haven't thought that far ahead. Been trying not to think about it at all. And failing miserably. "He . . . wasn't comfortable here."

Elisabeth shook her head. "That's not the way it appeared to me."

"You weren't here during the entire visit."

"Then tell me about it."

Morgan didn't want to relive it. It was bad enough the first time. "Why was he here? He wouldn't tell me."

"I'm not sure why he came, but once he was here, all he wanted to do was hear about you and Tyler."

"It doesn't make any sense. Why?"

Her mother chuckled softly. "You've been alone too long to see the signs? The man is interested in you."

Not in the way you think, Mom. He isn't looking for love and a family. Maybe a little fun on the side but nothing more. Nothing real. "But I'm not interested in him."

"Really? Then why did you kick him out?"

That's the easy one to answer. "He wasn't prepared for wha—"

"No sweetheart. You weren't prepared."

Her mother knew her so well that even when she didn't want to see the truth, her mother did, and was never afraid to let her know. Not harshly, but as a dear loving friend. And the truth was, she wasn't prepared. There was so much running through her mind. Good, bad, happy, and sad. For the last six years, the only emotion she'd allowed herself was the love she shared with her family. Everything else she'd put in a box, one she thought she'd never open again. How did Shaun lift the lid in only a week? What was it about him that was so different? And could she close the lid now? Was it too late to go back to the way things were just a week ago? A time when life may not have been easy, yet it was simple, and she was happy. That was more than she could say now. It felt painful to even think about smiling, never mind actually doing it.

Morgan buried her face in her hands, trying to shield the evidence of tears coming down. It wasn't about facing Shaun or any of the other Hendersons. It was all about her. She was trying to face things she'd avoided up to now. All she needed was one more day, and she knew she could pull herself together. *Just one more day.*

"I can't . . ." *face the world right now. I want to hide my head in the sand.*

"Then don't. Call your office and tell them you're ill."

Call out sick? I can't do that. Morgan wiped her cheeks and got up from the kitchen table. Giving up or giving in wasn't who she was. It was time to remember what was important to her, and that was Tyler's happiness and well-being.

Tyler came into the kitchen and sat down quietly at the table, waiting for his fruit bowl and toast. No matter what occurred, he went through the routine of his everyday life. She needed to be more like him, more resilient. *God, I love this boy. If only everyone could see him through my eyes. He's precious.*

Her decision was made. Today wasn't about going to face Shaun. This was about facing herself. Walter had left her filled with fear and insecurities. It was time to start becoming the woman she was before, strong and confident. It's what she wanted and what Tyler deserved. She never realized she was letting Walter win by hiding away like she was ashamed and defeated. There was no reason to feel ashamed and worthless. If anyone should feel that way, it should be the Sapp family.

Time to become an advocate. I've spent too many years avoiding the pain. Today it stops. You can't feel joy without dealing with some hurt.

"Mom, I'll be back by six." *If not earlier.*

"Where are you going?"

To do something I should have done from day one. Be myself. Be Morgan, the proud mama of an awesome young man, Tyler. "Work."

Morgan kissed Tyler on top of his head and walked out of the kitchen. She stopped in the hall and lifted one of the pictures off the wall. *I have the perfect spot on my desk for this.*

"WHAT DO YOU mean you weren't the one who authorized the change?"

"Dean, all I know is the contract changes never crossed my desk." Shaun didn't want to cause more concern than needed, but then again, Dean and Tessa didn't need another year like the prior one. He'd do whatever he needed to make sure no one hurt them again.

Dean picked up the phone. "Ask . . . the new woman in HR to come up here."

"Her name's Morgan."

"I don't care what her name is; I just need to make

sure she pulls her weight."

He knew Dean could be tough, but this was more like the old Dean, before Tessa. If anything, he thought Dean would come back from Paris more lenient. *What aren't you telling me? I can't help what I don't know.*

"She's better than I gave her credit for."

"That's not hard. I believe you thought she wasn't capable of anything. One day of training with Lexi was all she had. Even I thought I'd be getting calls from the staff saying they weren't paid."

It was closer than you think, but she pulled it off. That and many other things. He wasn't about to discuss Morgan with Dean or anyone else. He'd told her all his questions had been answered, but that was bullshit. When she'd practically demanded he leave her home, his list of questions quadrupled. He'd been tempted to stay and dig deeper, but not with her son there. He just needed to be patient, and she would come to him. *Never thought I'd look forward to a Monday morning.*

"Shaun, what's going on? You look . . . distracted." Dean arched a brow, eyeing him closely.

"I pulled Bennett in to do some research. He said he'd have the information this morning. That's all that's on my mind right now. I think that would be your top priority as well."

Dean got up from behind his desk. "It's one of them."

"What's the other?"

He ran his hand through his hair. "Shaun, Tessa is

pregnant."

Damn. "I thought you'd be happy about that."

"Mixed feelings."

I hope you haven't told Tessa that, otherwise I think the wedding will be off. Shaun wasn't the one to talk to Dean about family responsibilities. Hell, he didn't have any of his own. Morgan even picked up on his lack of experience Saturday. *I should tell you to talk to Brice. At least he's a father. Me, I'm just an asshole. And if you don't believe me, just ask Morgan.*

"I hear that's natural."

"Nothing about this family is natural. All I can do is think about our dad—what he was like. If I'm even a tenth of the man he was, I shouldn't be a father."

That's something I think about every day myself. "You're not. If you were, Tessa wouldn't be alive today would she? Good ole Dad never would've taken a bullet, never mind three, for any of us."

"Are you telling me that's not why you keep your distance? Why you've never married or never seriously dated anyone?"

Shaun didn't answer. It was a common fear they all shared. He could say otherwise, but Dean wasn't going to buy it.

There was no talking Dean out of how he felt about being a father. "This isn't about me. This is about you and Tessa, and now your child. Whatever doubts you have, you better get them under control quickly because whether you think you're fit or not, you're going to be a father."

There was a knock on the door, which meant their conversation would need to be tabled for now. *If I'm lucky, this will be the end of it.*

"Hello, Mr. Henderson. You asked to see me?"

Morgan entered and looked at Dean directly. *Avoiding me are you? Try if you want, but trust me Morgan, you'll find it's impossible.* She was back to dressing and acting pure business. No matter what she wore, she was beautiful, but he enjoyed how she looked Saturday. Her long hair loose and wild and dressed casually, playful. *More herself.*

"Call me Dean. Close the door and have a seat. I want to touch base regarding your first week."

Shaun almost laughed as he watched her stroll right over to the chair next to him and sit so she was facing Dean. *Why all the resistance when I ask?*

She was holding her laptop. "Would you like me to log into the system? I wasn't sure exactly what you might require this morning."

Dean shook his head. "If there were any problems, I would've already heard them from Shaun. Not sure if you've noticed, but he has no problem voicing his opinion."

Shaun watched Morgan smile slightly, but she gave no response. *Ever the professional. But I've seen the fiery side. I must bring out the fire in you. I hope so.*

"So what information can I provide you?"

Dean leaned forward to rest his arms on the desk.

"We didn't speak much before I left on my trip. The only training you received was from Lexi. Although she did a great job, I wanted to make sure you didn't have any questions about your position here."

"No. I'm clear on my responsibilities. And if I'm correct, the HR manager will be back today?"

"Not this week. She's pretty tired from the trip." Dean looked at Shaun then to Morgan. "I'd appreciate if this information does not leave this room."

"Of course," Morgan agreed.

"She's pregnant."

Morgan's face shined with a genuine glow of happiness for them. "Congratulations. I have a son who's nine. I wouldn't change being a parent for anything."

"There's nothing about it you'd change?" Shaun asked. It was what he was thinking, but he'd never expected it to come out. By the look on her face, he never should've voiced it.

Her beautiful honey brown eyes darkened. It wasn't anger he saw, but pain. Neither had been his intention. Normally he had full control of both his actions and words. Something about Morgan made him forget himself. *I'm not sure I like that.*

Although she was trying hard, Shaun could see her lip tremble as she spoke to him.

"I'm sure we all have things in our lives that we wish we could change. Some years ago and then some just last week. Wouldn't you agree?"

"I don't regret last week, Morgan." *Well, maybe the*

fact that it ended so soon. "Actually, I'm looking forward to more of the same this week."

She blushed. Out of the corner of his eye, he saw Dean lean back in his chair, observing. *Don't put too much into this, Dean. I'm just having a little bit of fun, and that's all. Nothing more.*

"Did I come back too early? Seems like the two of you worked *very* well together. Would you like me to go away again?"

"No," Morgan answered.

Dean laughed. "And here I thought she found you charming, Shaun."

Shaun wasn't laughing at all. He knew what Dean was trying to do, and it wasn't going to happen. He was more than willing to enjoy some time with Morgan, but that was as far as it was going. Once alone, he would set him straight.

Morgan looked embarrassed as she tried to cover up her blatant rejection of Dean's offer.

"That's not what I meant. It's just I . . . am sure your brother has his own work to do and I . . . really . . ."

"Dean, you do have a lot on your plate. Right now I can handle the HR and finance side while you catch up on the production and contracts." Shaun couldn't believe he was offering to assist longer than he already had. He had never worked closely with his brothers before. It went smoothly for a week, but any longer and it could blow up in both their faces. So why did he say that? *Because I wanted to see her reaction, and it's just as I expected. Happy but wishing she wasn't. She wants to see me again, but for some reason she won't admit it. Let's see if I can remedy that.*

Dean nodded to him but said, "Let's just make it HR for now. I want to keep a close eye on the finance department too, since it links so closely with the contracts."

Shaun should've thought of that. Until they heard from Bennett, those two departments had red flags on them.

"Since that is settled, Morgan, why don't you follow me to my office next door? We can leave Dean to finish playing catch-up."

She didn't move, clearly not wanting to acknowledge him. From his angle he could see her eyes were wide open as though still in shock. "I have some things I need to attend to in my office. Can we make it another time?"

He resisted the temptation to tell her no. Let her know there was some imperative business for them to discuss behind closed doors. "This afternoon would work for me. I'll have Britany-Lynn schedule it."

He couldn't help himself as he watched her leave the office. The sway of her hips enticed him to follow, but he and Dean still had business to discuss. Morgan would have to wait.

"Oh yeah. Keeping a close eye on the HR Department is really going to suck isn't it, Shaun?"

Shaun caught the sarcasm but didn't care. He'd expected nothing less when he made the offer. Dean didn't need his help any more than he needed Dean's.

"How about we get back to business."

"You're the boss. Of HR that is." Once again more laughter.

Oh, I hope you don't tell Zoey. If she finds out, I'm never going to hear the end of it. His phone rang. *Perfect. Just what I've been waiting for.*

"Bennett, you're on speaker with Dean and me. What did you find out?"

"Welcome back, Dean. Shaun, as I told you last week, this does not feel like a threat in any way. I ran all the background checks again, and your entire staff is clean. I looked extra deep into Donald's background. That kid is as clean as they come."

"So it took you the weekend to come up with nothing?" Shaun slammed him.

"Not exactly. You'd asked me to look into Morgan. And at that time I was resistant," Bennett stated.

What the hell did you find out Bennett? Is she a mole? Is that why I can't get her out of my mind? "And now?"

"From what I can find, she's the only person who could've doctored those contracts. Why, is the mystery I'm still digging into."

Fuck. Why her? None of this made sense. How is it that someone who works in HR could handle writing a contract better than the contract specialist?

"What else do you know about her?" Shaun asked.

"She worked for WS & Son about six years ago. I spoke to the owner, and he confirmed she worked as their senior contract manager. She left abruptly without notice, and he had nothing nice to say about her. Actually, brutal would be the words he used. He wouldn't give me any details, but his exact words were, 'I never want to hear her name again.' I'll keep digging if you want to see if she ever filed an unemployment claim against them."

That sounded like one hell of a termination/resignation. What happened between them didn't matter, except she was now here at Poly-Shyn. He wasn't going to allow this to be round two for her. He needed to know so he could determine what actions to take. "He gave no indication why she left?"

"None. Something's off on this. I can feel it. But either way, I still don't believe she's a threat to Poly-Shyn or any of the family. I think what went down at WS & Son is probably none of our business."

"If she's working here, then I'm making it my business. I don't care what rock you need to look under. Find me everything. I'll determine what is or isn't our business."

When he disconnected the call with Bennett, he looked at Dean, who for the first time looked like he was taking this seriously.

"Why wouldn't she apply for a contract position?"

Shaun shook his head. "Why wouldn't she mention she was reviewing contracts here? It's not part of her job description, so why do it, unless you have an agenda which we have yet to discover."

"Let's get her out of here now."

"No. Let me handle this. There's more to her than she leads us to believe. I want to know what that is." Shaun thought he understood when he stopped at her home. Obviously, that was not the only thing she'd been keeping a secret. *And I want to know why.*

"Okay, but I'm going to tell Tessa to stay out of the office until this is handled. I don't want anything stressing her right now. And if she thinks there could be someone out to mess with us again . . . well, that's not good for her or the baby."

Shaun agreed. *And look at you, already being a good father.*

Chapter Eight

MORGAN HAD WAITED all Monday for Shaun to contact her, but he didn't. Then Tuesday and Wednesday much of the same. If he thought she was going to give in and contact him, he didn't know who he was dealing with. *Doesn't mean I don't want to; it just means I won't.*

It was almost four thirty when he finally emailed her to meet with him in ten minutes. That was going to mean cutting it close for dinner with Tyler.

The first thing she did was call her mother and warn her she probably was going to be late.

"A date?" Elisabeth asked, sounding hopeful.

"Work."

Each day she asked Morgan if she'd spoken to Shaun. Every time she said no. It looked like tonight was going to be a different answer. *Unfortunately.*

While chatting with her mother, Morgan shot back a message asking Shaun if they could meet first thing in the morning. One-word response. *No.*

"I can't believe the balls that man has."

"And whom are you speaking about, Morgan?"

She'd forgotten her mother was still on the phone. She explained about the last-minute meeting Shaun had just scheduled.

"This is nothing new. You worked late all the time when you worked for . . . the other company. Why are you so upset with this request? Were you hoping it would be a dinner invitation instead?"

"Mom, there is nothing going on between us. This is a business meeting only."

"If you say so."

"I do. I'm just upset because he knows damn well I have a son waiting at home for me. Just because he doesn't have any responsibilities, doesn't mean the rest of us don't." She closed her laptop and headed to her meeting while still chatting with her mother on her cell phone. "I don't want to work with him, or for him." Morgan blurted out as she waited for the elevator.

When the door opened she told her mother she had to go. There was a positive side to working on that floor alone, she could say what she wanted and no one could rat her out, but that wasn't the case throughout the building.

Of course, that was all going to change once Tessa returned. *I remember those early months when I was carrying Tyler. I was so tired I could hardly lift my head from the pillow. And if anyone even looked at me oddly, I burst into tears. Yep, things are going to change once she's back in the office.*

She was happy for them even though she really didn't know either of them. Just hearing how much they loved each other touched her heart. *I hope it lasts for them because it really sucks when you watch all your dreams go down the tubes.*

Morgan hated that her actions these last few days were still driven by hurt from many years ago. How long was it going to take for her to let it go? Move on? *Maybe if it was just me Walter hurt, I could be more forgiving. But he did it to our son, and that is a wound that won't ever go away. And I don't want to forget. If I do, then I'll only risk it happening again. I'm not sure either Tyler or I can survive another hit like that.*

No matter how she tried, she couldn't stop thinking of Shaun. Was this his plan all along? *He must be trying to see if he can get a reaction out of me. Well, he can try, but I know how to handle myself.*

Morgan remembered how she handled herself last week. She could've pushed him away when he kissed her. *Truthfully, I'm a grown woman. I could've stopped it even before the kiss. But I didn't. I wanted him to kiss me. And I want him to kiss me again.*

She got off the elevator and headed down the hall to face the one person who turned her world upside down. It wasn't work that worried her, it was herself. *And I can't run from that.*

Without thinking, she knocked on Dean's office in error.

"Sorry. I was looking for Shaun."

"Why don't you come in for a minute and shut the door." Dean waved her to the seat opposite him.

Is he going to fire me? Is that why Shaun waited until the end of the day? That's standard in the industry. She did as Dean asked and sat quietly, waiting. She could feel her cheeks still flushed from the thoughts of Shaun. The last thing she needed was Dean or anyone else picking up the wrong vibe. *This is what I get for fantasizing at work. Now I feel like I'm in the principal's office and about to get a lecture on being a lady.*

"I know I said you would be reporting to Shaun, but it's Wednesday, and I want to make sure there are no issues I should know about."

Oh, there are, but none that I'm about to share with you or anyone else.

"Things are going fine from what I can tell."

"I didn't mean with the job; I meant with reporting to Shaun. I noticed on Monday there seemed to be some . . . tension between you two."

She couldn't bring herself to look at Dean, even though she felt his eyes on her the entire time. Was it her cold behavior that Dean had picked up on? *Obviously. He's talking to you about it now, isn't he?*

"I'm sorry. I'll be more professional in the future."

Dean gave her a puzzled look. "It's not you I'm worried about."

Oh, I think you're wrong there. You should worry about us both. "Believe me, Mr. Henderson."

"Dean."

"Dean, believe me. Working under Shaun will not affect my work at all."

He arched a brow, and she knew he was trying to read her. Morgan wasn't going to give him anything this time.

"If that is all, I have a meeting now with Shaun, and I don't want to be late." She got up from the chair and made her way to the door. She knew he was still watching even as she turned the knob. *Dean didn't buy that at all, did he?*

When she decided to come to the office on Monday, it was to face her own fear. Maybe fear wasn't the word she'd been avoiding. *Want. Lust. Desire. Yep. These sound more like it.*

Even when she found Shaun sitting in her mother's home, she couldn't help but be attracted to him. Of course, that only pissed her off more than his surprise visit. And now, for some reason, she seemed to be wearing her childish crush—or whatever it was—on her sleeve for everyone to see. This had to stop. He was the brother of the owner. There was no way he would be interested in her. And if he was, it wasn't going to be anything more than a romp in the sack. *Not interested in that at all.*

Before she knocked on the correct door, she took a deep inhale and made a slow exhale. *Nope, not one bit.*

"Come in."

Control Morgan. Stay in control and remember, this is business only, just like I told Mom. Only business.

She'd seen him many times in the hall. He was always dressed in an expense suit. When you had his kind of money, why not? This afternoon he was dressed in a pair of jeans that hugged his hips just right. Instead of a stuffy shirt, he was wearing a T-shirt that showed off his biceps. *Only business. Only business.*

"Close the door and come sit by me."

Only business. Oh shit. I'm screwed.

BENNETT HAD TOLD him he'd find out what happened, but Shaun wasn't a man with a lot of patience. He could go back and talk to Elisabeth as she seemed to be very forthcoming. Why go around snooping when he had the source right here?

She was sitting, her legs crossed tight as though he was going to try to get inside them. *Not that I haven't given that a lot of thought, but right now, I have something else on my mind. Finding out more about you.*

She opened her laptop, and he said, "Close it."

Morgan shut it but looked puzzled. "We are here for our HR meeting, correct?"

"HR questions to be more precise."

I know what I know, but not anything beyond that. So if this is a test on my qualifications, it's going to be a short meeting. "Keep in mind that I'm new to this department."

"Oh, I know. But why is more my question."

She had no idea what that meant. *I'm new because I was only hired last week.* "I believe you *were* there the day

I was hired."

"I want to know why you took a job in HR."

I ask myself that every day. Same answer. Because I was offered it. "I enjoy it."

"But that is not your specialty. Wouldn't you agree?"

He was fishing for something. She could feel it. But why? And what? "No, it's not."

"Then again I ask: why HR? Why not another department where you might be more qualified?"

Is he just playing a game with me right now? Because these questions are too vague to answer correctly. "This is the one I was offered."

"So you wouldn't rather be in the file room or maybe in corporate contracts?"

Damn it, Donald. You weren't supposed to say anything. How do I explain this now? "I like where I am right now."

He didn't sit. Only stood with his arms folded, staring at her.

"Shaun, if you have questions just ask, because I need to get home."

He came closer, and leaned back on his desk. Now he was only a foot away from her. She wished he would get back up and pace or something; this closeness wasn't going to help her keep in control of anything, never mind her responses.

"Tell me about WS & Son."

Her heart almost stopped. That was a name she never put on a résumé. How did he find out? Was he digging into her past? Boston had its own business world, so it was possible someone she worked with there, was now here.

"They are located on the other side of Boston. They are not a competitor of Poly-Shyn, if that is what you are worried about."

"Why did you leave?" His eyes were burning into her now as though he could detect her reluctance to answer just through her pulse.

So many things came to mind. But only one was going to appease him even slightly. It was a half-truth, so maybe this would stop the questioning. There was only so much she was going to tell him as none of it was his business.

"I wanted to be home with Tyler." Her answer was simple and over. Now she sat and waited.

"Morgan, I'm asking you to tell me what happened. What made you leave a senior contract management position practically overnight?" His voice wasn't demanding or accusing as she thought it would be.

Do you really want to know why? How will you knowing they hurt Tyler and me benefit our working relationship any?

"Please, Morgan."

She was lost at the honest request. This was a side of him she'd never seen before. But she wasn't ready to tell him. It was a private part of her that she'd buried and wanted to keep there. Now he was in front of her, asking her to open it all up again.

"Shaun, I can't."

"Can't or won't, Morgan?"

"What's the difference? It doesn't have anything to do with my job here."

"I'm not talking about work. I want to know what happened."

Why are you being so . . . I don't know, caring? Understanding? Friendly? You won't be once you hear what went down and how I left. I wasn't professional at all. I reacted not acted. My emotions ran rampant. I don't want you to know that person. "We had a huge difference of opinions that we couldn't reconcile. So I moved on." Everything inside of her wanted to break as though she were a teacup coming in contact with a tile floor. No matter how she tried to hide it, her hands were trembling, and her voice was shaky.

I need to get out of here to pull myself together. You caught me off guard with the one thing I'm never going to be prepared to talk about.

He said nothing but moved from where he'd been leaning and went to sit behind his desk.

Morgan asked, hoping to get out before he asked any more questions that she didn't want to answer, "Is that all?" She felt the plea for release bubbling within her. *Please don't let my desperation be evident to him. I don't want him knowing how weak I am.*

Shaun nodded. "Have a good night."

Morgan held her laptop more tightly than she thought possible without breaking it, and bolted out of the office. She wanted to get home, but not as much as she wanted to put some miles between her and Shaun. *Maybe I should reach out to Dean and let him know reporting to Shaun was going to be impossible. He's . . . he's making me think of things, and I don't want to. He's looking at me as though he really cares. If he knew the truth, he wouldn't, and Dean would probably agree.*

She didn't stop in her office to drop off her laptop. It was coming home with her tonight. Right now she needed out of that building. *And if I'm lucky, I'll still make it home for Tyler. That's where I belong.*

SHAUN DIDN'T HAVE any more details than he'd started with before the meeting. The one thing that was clear, though, was this wasn't an ordinary difference of opinions. Something serious went down between her and that company. Whatever it was, it left her feeling . . . defeated? Angry? No, it was deeper. He couldn't put his finger on it.

Pulling out his cell, he called Bennett.

"Any update?"

"I just entered the building and am on my way up to see you."

"Good, I'm in my office. I want to hear this alone and will decide what Dean needs to know," Shaun barked.

He expected a smart ass remark, but he got something else instead. "Shaun, mark this day on your calendar, because for the first time I agree with you."

Shaun didn't like the sound of that. He knew there was something, but now it sounded as though it was much more personal than he'd expected. *Maybe Bennett is right and what happened at WS & Son is none of my business. But I need to know what caused her to be hurt like she was.*

That was it. She wasn't defeated. She'd been hurt, broken by it. *I have to know.*

His mind was running on overdrive, and it was pissing him off. Bennett was on his way up and had the answers, all he needed to do was wait a few minutes. He'd been on the edge of deals worth millions of dollars and never lost a wink of sleep. What the hell was wrong with him now?

The door was still open from when Morgan left, so he hadn't even heard Bennett enter.

"Morgan looked like hell leaving the building a few minutes ago. Did you have anything to do with that?" Bennett asked as he made his way to sit on the couch.

All me. He'd pushed her but not as far as he could've. If it'd been any other person, they'd have been stuck in that office until he had exactly what he wanted. But he saw her pleading brown eyes. They reminded him of Zoey after their father had punished her. They would ask her what happened, and that was all they got. The look that says the pain was more than she could bear. He knew he should go after her, make sure she was okay. He should tell her he was sorry for bringing it up. But the truth was, he wasn't sorry. He was glad to see this side of her. She shared it with him even though she might not know it. At any time, she could have gotten up and walked out of his office. But she didn't. *She wants to talk about it. She just doesn't know how.*

"Let's get down to business. What did you find?"

Bennett nodded. He knew when not to cross the line. That's why he was so beneficial to the Hendersons. Sometimes he was used for business and other times things were not his business, but they still needed his help. He understood the lines without anyone needing to clarify them for him.

"Let's start with saying once again, she's not here as a threat in any way to Poly-Shyn."

"I agree with you on that. But right now all I want to know is what the fuck went down at WS & Son?" Shaun's voice filled with anger as he demanded answers. Bennett never flinched. *Another reason why you're invaluable. You're not intimidated by anyone, Henderson or not.*

"You'd better sit. This is going to take a while if you want everything I found out."

Shaun sat in the armed leather chair across from Bennett. Whatever it was, he'd be there for Morgan, help her through dealing with it, because he knew it still troubled her.

"Start high-level then we'll dig into the weeds if I say we need to." Shaun was good at picking out what information was important and what wasn't. It was the edge he used to be successful. See things before the competition.

"Do you know she has a child?"

Shaun nodded. "Yes, Tyler. I met him last Saturday."

Bennett raised a brow. "Maybe you should start by telling me what you know."

"No." Although what he had was helpful, Elisabeth gave him only the information she wanted to.

"Okay. She, as you know, has a nine-year-old boy, Tyler. She's raised him alone since the age of three. But if you ask me, it was since birth because she never lived with the father."

Single mom. Tough job. But that didn't cause the pain in her eyes. It was more than just that. "Tell me about the father."

Shaun had only wanted to know what happened at the job; now he was totally invading her privacy. He should stop, but he wasn't going to. Something in him wanted to know everything about her.

"It's all linked, Shaun. The entire fucking story is linked to that bastard."

For the first time, he saw Bennett's anger. If this information was setting him off, then God knows what it was going to do to him.

"Tyler's father is Walter Sapp, Jr. He is the son in WS & Son."

Shaun had done some digging into the company, and they might not be his competition, but they weren't chump change either. The company's last estimated worth was over eight hundred million. If he was the father, then why would Morgan and Tyler be living in an apartment and not a nice house someplace with a housekeeper and cook?

"Does Walter know he's the father?"

"Oh, that bastard knows. It wasn't easy getting information because the employees all fear they'll lose their jobs, but I have what you need."

"Let it rip."

"They were dating and pretty seriously. She was the senior contract manager and for damn good reasons. She was the top negotiator in pretty much every major deal they had. If it weren't for her, they wouldn't be where they are now. Of course, the payback for such loyalty ended as soon as the Sapps found out the child was autistic."

"What do you mean ended?"

"I mean the fucking asshole cut off all ties with her and Tyler. He actually accused her of cheating on him one day at work in front of a few of her staff members, saying there was no way that messed-up kid could be his. She quit that day and never went back."

The pain was starting to make sense now. "Why didn't she fight? Is it possible he was right?"

"No. She had a DNA test taken, which proved he was the father. He wouldn't respond to it. From what I hear, she went to his father, the owner, and had Tyler with her. She wanted him to see his grandchild. Let's just say, Junior's bad behavior was a carbon copy of his father's. He threw her out of his office and told her that he never wanted to see that little brat again. And from what I see, neither of them have contacted her or assisted her in any way."

His head was throbbing. If that bastard were there in front of him right now, Shaun would be going to jail for assault or worse. Until that moment, he never understood how Dean could've lost his temper and almost beat someone to death. It was taking everything in him to stay in control. If the man were anywhere close, he would show him what a fucking coward deserved for disrespecting women and children.

"I could keep digging, but I think you have what you need from me. Now you have to decide what you're going to do with this information." Bennett stood and walked to the door, but before leaving, he turned back to Shaun. "She's been through a lot, Shaun. Before you move any further into her life, make sure you're not going to be another asshole for her to add to the list. Because with everything I've found, she's not your average girl, if you know what I mean."

Shaun didn't like the warning, but he appreciated that Bennett cared enough for Morgan to give one.

Once alone he walked back to his desk, opened the drawer, and pulled out a glass and the bottle of bourbon he stored there for emergencies. He hadn't touched it since his father died. He hadn't needed to.

Leaning back in his chair, he pictured her face as he questioned her earlier. *Damn it. If I'd known before I never would've pressured her.*

Shaun wanted to tell her he understood what a mean

neglectful parent was all about, but he had no clue what she was feeling. To have a son you love and be accused of the things she'd been accused of, just because Tyler was different. *She's gone through so much. But she can't let an asshole like him rule her life forever. If she does, he wins. Never let them win.*

That's how he dealt with his own father. It was a horrible way to grow up, but in the end, no matter how hard his father had tried, he hadn't been able to break him. Morgan was an amazingly strong woman. He knew she had it in her to fight, to demand what was rightfully hers. She should never have needed to struggle to support Tyler when Walter had plenty of money to go around. So why didn't she? Why walk away and let him go on with his life as though she and Tyler never existed? If it were him, he'd be in there raking Walter's ass over the coals. *I'd make him wish he'd never heard of my name, for an entirely different reason than his child was autistic.*

There was a major difference between the two of them. She ran and hid. He wanted to teach her to fight back. Was that a good thing? Maybe not, but he didn't want to see her get hurt again. Not by Walter or anyone else.

He picked up his cell and scrolled for her number. Before he hit the call button, he thought about what he'd say. *Hey, just found out your son's father is an asshole. Want me to go and punch his lights out?*

Shaun decided this was going to require a different course of action. Getting up, he put the phone in his back pocket and left his office. Dean saw him as he shut the door.

"Was that Bennett I heard earlier?"

"Yeah. He came by with some information regarding Morgan."

"Want to come in and fill me in?"

"No. He was right the first time. She's not a threat to Poly-Shyn or anyone else. She's only here for a job. My suggestion is to let her stay and do it."

There was no need for Dean to know of her past. She had the right to her privacy. *Too bad I didn't respect it, but I needed to know. And I'm glad I do.*

"Does that mean you're vacating the office next door and going back to your own office?"

"Nope." Turning, he walked down the hall to call it a night. He had a lot of thinking to do and standing there talking to Dean wasn't going to get it done.

There wasn't much he needed in life right now. But one thing he knew, he needed to see her. As he got into his limo, he gave his driver her address. As they pulled away from the curb, Shaun said, "I've changed my mind. Take me home."

He was ready for the conversation, but he knew she wasn't. If he showed up unannounced, all she was going to do was kick his ass out again. He would see her and earn her trust. He could tell her he knew, but instead he wanted her to open up to him. He didn't know how long it was going to take, but he was willing to wait.

Looks like it's time for another weekend visit. Planned this time.

Chapter Nine

"HI, SHAUN. IF you're looking for Brice, he's in the office," Lena said when she opened the door.

"I'm actually here to talk to you."

Lena's look of surprise probably matched his own. Over the last eighteen months they only spoke during their once a month Sunday brunch at her house. *She's family. And probably the only one who can help me right now.*

"Come in. Nicholas is napping so let's sit in the kitchen, and I'll make some coffee."

He knew Zoey would kill him if she found out he came to talk to Lena instead of her, but Zoey didn't have the experience he required. And experience mattered most of all.

Lena poured a cup and took the seat across from him. She sat quietly, waiting for him to speak. He knew exactly what he wanted to ask, but now he wasn't sure where to start. If Brice were home, he would have to choose his words more carefully. Lena, on the other hand, was born to be a mom. She not only took care of their son, Nicholas, but she looked like she was about to deliver any day now. *Nice. Dean and Tessa's baby will have a cousin to play with. Which I better not mention, because I don't know who knows what.*

"Sometimes it's easier just to spit it out and let me do the rest."

"I need to ask you about children."

He'd shocked her for the second time in a matter of minutes. Her expression softened, and she smiled at him. "Is this your way of saying you're going to be a father?"

"Hell no." He didn't mean that to sound so sharp but being a father was the furthest thing from his mind.

"Okay, guess I was wrong. I'm going to need a little more information if you want my help."

Shaun gulped his hot coffee, not caring if it burned his mouth. *Okay. Let's get this over with.*

"I have a friend who has a child. My experience with children is . . . none. I have none. The only kid I've ever been around is Nicholas. He's easy because he's like you. You know. Happy."

"Thank you. But trust me. Nicholas is a lot like Brice."

"Sorry about that." Shaun tried to ease the subject with a bit of humor. That's the way his brother Alex handled every situation. He only hoped it worked as well when he tried. *No one's ever accused me of being funny. Not even a little bit.*

"So tell me about this friend of yours."

"Her name is Morgan. She has a son who is nine. I

just don't know what kids like to do, or what to do with them?"

"What's his name?"

"Tyler."

"Boys are so much easier than girls. You could go fishing or bowling or baseball. They like to be active."

"I may have left out one part that is important. But then again maybe not. Okay, I really know what is important when it comes to children, never mind this one. All I know is I don't want to hurt him."

Not hurting someone so innocent. What a concept. Maybe I'm not the carbon copy of my father. She must have.

Lena reached across the table and touched Shaun's hand. "Then you have exactly what he needs." Shaun looked at her. He had no idea what that was. "You care about him, Shaun. When you care enough about another person to avoid hurting them, then the rest is easy."

Easy. I didn't even know that I started to care. I just wanted to know what not to do. I don't want to be like Walter. I refuse to be like him. "He's autistic. How do you connect with him?"

"Morgan would be the best to tell you, as children or adults with special needs all react to things differently. Have you seen him do anything which might provide a hint of what he likes?"

I've only met him once. How can I know anything from that? He thought back to that day. What had Elisabeth told him? Had she provided a clue? *Yes! The bike ride.*

Shaun got up quickly. "Thanks, Lena."

"Wait! You're leaving that quickly?"

"Sorry. I have some shopping to do."

"By the smile on your face, you've got your answer." She stood and rubbed her well-rounded belly. "I'm happy for you. But can I offer one piece of advice?"

He stopped in his tracks and waited for her to slam him for even having the thought. Tell him that he shouldn't even think about entering into a child's life. That he was not fit to be around them.

"What is that?"

"Talk to Morgan. Because if I'm right, and I usually am about these things, you're not just interested in understanding Tyler better, but more like both of them. And I'm sure she'd want to know that. I know I would if I were in her shoes."

He had every intention of getting to know Morgan, but no plans of talking to her about it. Nope he was going to handle her his own way. *Women I understand. Well, as best as any man can I guess, which is not at all. Oh, fuck.* "This is going to get so damn complicated isn't it?"

Lena laughed. "Oh, the battle of the sexes can be so much fun. As, long as you understand one thing."

"What is that?"

"That winning isn't everything." She reached up on tippy toes and gave him a kiss on the cheek. "That's for good luck. Don't worry. I won't say anything to your brother."

"Thank you."

He left and was actually happy he'd stopped instead of just calling on the phone. He didn't spend enough time with the family. *That's another thing that needs to change. But one thing at a time. Right now, it's all about Morgan and Tyler.*

He was going to make plans for this Saturday with them. He only hoped she was going to be open to what he'd planned. *No risk, no glory.*

When he got back in the limo he told the driver to take him to a bicycle shop. The driver looked over his shoulder with a puzzled look as though he hadn't heard correctly.

"And make it one that carries a bicycle built for three."

A smile came over the driver's face, which usually remained emotionless. He couldn't know what he'd planned. Then he remembered how he'd stayed outside while Shaun had been inside talking to Elisabeth. He would've seen the same thing he did. *The bicycle built for two. Oh. I'm going to need to remember you're much more aware of what's going on than I give you credit for. Not sure I like that.*

THIS WEEK WAS so much better than the last. With one exception: Shaun's little interrogation. Morgan had thought for sure he'd try again, but he never mentioned anything. They were even in the same meeting this week, and he'd treated her like any other employee. *Not saying that's a good thing, but at least we're past what awkward-*

ness there was.

That didn't mean she felt any different. When she looked at him she secretly hoped he'd be looking at her. Each time she was disappointed. Why? She told him no, and he was respecting that. She should be happy. But she wasn't. She pushed him away, but she still wanted him. *How is he supposed to know what I want, when I don't know myself?*

The truth was she still didn't know. She'd talked it out with her mother who'd given her wonderful advice. None of which she'd taken because times had changed since her parents were dating. Besides, she and Shaun weren't dating. They weren't anything. *And that's the problem. We're in this limbo. I think I'd rather have him barking orders at me and giving me a cold stare than this lack of emotion. This sucks. Why can't he be the miserable one instead of me?*

She finished the email she was working on and checked it for errors. *What the hell?* The first line said, "Sorry for your incontinence," instead of "Sorry for your inconvenience." She hit delete on the email. *And this is a good indication that nothing productive is going to get done right now.*

Instead of trying to refocus, she decided to ride out the remaining time. When she looked at the clock, it was much later than she'd thought. Smiling, she sat back and began watching the second hand on the wall clock tick away. *Why is it the last five minutes on Friday seem to drag?* Her mother always told her a watched pot never boils.

Must apply to clocks too.

As soon as it was five, she shut down her laptop and rushed home. Thankfully, she beat all the traffic and before she knew it, she was pulling into the driveway. Her mother came rushing out with Tyler by her side. There was a grin on her face that said trouble.

"Oh, Morgan. I can't wait till you see it."

She was tired and didn't want to play the game. "See what, Mom?"

Elisabeth grabbed her hand and pulled her to the side of the garage. There she saw a silver and green bike. Okay, nice. So they got a new bike. She couldn't understand why so much drama for a bike. It's not like they don't each have one already. "Whose bike? Yours or Dad's?"

"Yours."

"Mine? I have a bike, Mom. You know that. What do I need with another one? Besides, I never ride alone. Only with Tyler."

"I know that. And I think someone else does too." Elisabeth was almost dancing with excitement. "Go see it."

Someone gave me a bike they know I don't need? Well, that's just special. Morgan knew her mother wasn't going to let her inside the house until she went and did the official *oh, wow.* As she walked closer to the bike, her mother was all bubbly. This wasn't just any bike, but one built for three. *Who the hell would get me something like this?*

The neighbors all knew Tyler and she rode each Saturday. Maybe one of them or a bunch of them got together to get her this. She didn't know much about bikes, but she knew this one was very expensive, as she'd looked at it so she could go riding with Tyler and her mother. "Who? Why?"

Elisabeth nudged her from behind. "Go read the card and find out."

Mom, you know very well that you've already done that. At thirty-six, I think I've figured a few things out by now. "Mom. I'm exhausted. Can't you just tell me what it says?"

"Oh I could, but I won't."

And we're friends why? Oh yeah, because you're awesome, most of the time. Morgan went to where the bow was and saw a white envelope. It wasn't sealed, but that wouldn't have stopped her mother. Slowly she pulled out the note.

"See you Saturday at ten a.m. I'd like to get to know Tyler better. Looking forward to spending the day with you both."

It wasn't signed, and the handwriting wasn't familiar. *I have no idea who's coming. Could it be Walter has changed his mind and now wants to see Tyler? No, even if he had, he'd never do something so publicly as to ride a bike through the streets with him. He's made it very clear what an embarrassment Tyler is to him. So if not Walter, then who?*

When she turned around holding the card, her

mother said, "Can you believe it? When I told him about your weekly bike ride I never thought he'd want to join in. But I guess he does."

"Who does?"

"Shaun, silly."

Shaun? Did he send this bike? Is he coming tomorrow? What does he want? Didn't we just do this last week and I kicked him out? Why's he coming back for more of the same?

She brushed past her mother and started toward the house.

"Are you running off to call and thank him?" Elisabeth teased.

Not hardly, I'm calling the bike shop to get this thing out of my yard. She dialed the number and received voice mail saying the store was closed for the weekend and they'd open again on Monday morning. *Great. Just great.*

"Now what am I supposed to do?"

Her mother, who'd followed her inside, replied, "Simple. Go for the ride with him tomorrow."

She turned and gave her mother a warning look. Morgan didn't play around when it came to Tyler. Going for a ride with the two of them could end badly. Shaun didn't understand anything about Tyler. It wasn't so much about the ride as much as following a routine. They left at the same time and always took the same path. *What's Tyler going to do when he sees a different bike? Even a slight change like that can trigger a meltdown in him. Tomorrow is too late to try to explain that to Shaun. Damn it.*

"Mom, can you please watch Tyler for a few minutes? I want to go upstairs and call Shaun." *Not for the reason you think, so don't get your hopes up.*

"Take your time. I'll finish dinner while the two of you chat."

Once inside her apartment, she pulled her cell phone out and dialed his business cell as that was all she had. She wasn't sure if he'd answer after hours, but he struck her as the type of man who never wanted to miss a business opportunity.

"Henderson here."

Part of her was hoping she'd get voice mail and get away with leaving a message. "Hi, Shaun, it's Morgan."

"How are you?"

Stressed to the max thanks to you. But that seems to be the pattern with you now, doesn't it? "Concerned. Confused."

There was a pause then he asked, "Why concerned?"

At least, you understand why I'm confused. We're halfway there. "I received a bike today. I take it that was from you?"

"Yes."

"Although it was a nice gesture, I cannot accept it."

"Why not?"

A long sigh had escaped before she continued, "You don't understand anything about autism do you?"

"No, enlighten me."

"This isn't something I can talk to you about over the phone. You can google it. Take a class on it. But talking to you about Tyler and how something like this might affect him on the phone won't really make the point I'm trying to get at."

"Easy to remedy. Have dinner with me."

What? That's not the point I was trying to make either. "We're going to be eating at six. Once again, it's about routine."

"Fine. Eat light, and I can pick you up once he goes to bed."

You are so not getting it. How can someone so brilliant be so damn dumb. "Shaun, you don't seem to understand me."

"I do. But I want to see you. If you don't want to have dinner, then we can have drinks."

"Why?"

"Because I want to see you. And because I want to learn what to do when I'm around Tyler, so I don't mess with the routine you're talking about."

Why do you need to be so logical? Don't you know my thoughts of you are not logical at all? Not even appropriate if you ask anyone in HR. Oh, that would be me. No matter what her brain was telling her, her heart screamed yes. Which seemed to be ruling her lips as she heard her voice agreeing and even setting a time.

"Pick me up at ten."

When she ended the call she knew she now had to face the second person she didn't want to tonight. *Mom, I don't want you making this anything more than what it is. We're only meeting to talk about Tyler. Nothing more.*

Part of her was disappointed even as she thought it. But this was needed so he could understand why he needed to back off. Why he couldn't be part of their lives. *He doesn't fit. And I need to show him that. No matter how much I wish he did, he doesn't and never will.*

Chapter Ten

S HE HAD NO idea why she let her mother talk her into wearing a dress. And one that was form fitting. After all her talk about how this wasn't a date, she sure looked like she was on one now.

He was prompt and picked her up at exactly ten. They were polite the entire ride to the restaurant. *Right now this isn't feeling like a date either. Maybe I have nothing to worry about. Maybe this is exactly what he said; he wants to learn about Tyler.*

Over dinner, she told him everything she knew from years of raising a child with autism. How there is a vast autism spectrum, from very high functioning cases who work and raise families, to very low functioning cases who will never be able to live on their own unsupervised. Most of the information she gave him was based around Tyler specifically, but she added some general information he could use if he met anyone else with autism.

"I am very fortunate to have my mother watch him for me when he's not in school. I don't know how I would do it without her and my dad."

She regretted saying it and closed her eyes, hoping that didn't open the door for him to ask about Walter. For a moment she was sure he was going to because his expression changed so quickly. He opened his mouth, but closed it again. *Being a gentleman? I like that. I'm far from ready to tell you about him, and I might not ever be.*

"So that's a crash course of what I know from my personal experience. There is much more. But hopefully you understand why I was so concerned about the bike. And, we cannot accept such an expensive gift."

To him money was no object, but she lived much differently. Things would be easier since she had an office job again, but she couldn't count on that lasting forever. Shaun had already questioned her about her old job. Once he found out she walked off without any notice at all, he wouldn't want her on staff for very long.

Shaun ignored her last comment. "I never realized how simple changes could affect him so much. I hope you know that was not my intention when I sent the bike."

There was so much she didn't know about Shaun, but she did know he'd never hurt her son intentionally. Actually, she couldn't picture him hurting any child or elderly person. He might not admit it, but he was a softy. He remembered what Tyler liked and then went out of his way to find something he believed would make him happy. He hadn't said it, but she wanted to hear it. So she used one of her mother's lines and asked a question that she already knew the answer to.

"Why did you buy it, Shaun?"

He looked into her eyes and said, "I told you. I wanted to get to know both of you better. The only thing I knew about Tyler was you two went on a ride together each Saturday. I thought it might be a good place to start."

Oh, my God. That's so sweet, so touching. I could kiss you. But I won't because we're not out on a date. This is about Tyler only. Remember that. Tyler only. Not a date.

"You didn't need to buy a bike for that. You could've just asked, and I would've told you."

Shaun reached out across the table and touched her hand. A chill ran up her, and her body reacted more than she could hide. She felt flushed and not from embarrassment. *Not what I want in a public restaurant. Why is your timing always off, Shaun? First at the office and now here. Didn't you ever read the dating manual? You pick up the girl, take her out, kiss her goodnight on her door stoop in the moonlight.*

Morgan almost laughed out loud at her own thoughts. *I think I should read that manual; I'm so out of practice. It's been six years. Six very long years.* Up until now she had never given it a thought. Her life was full, not lacking. But being with him made her feel differently. She wanted to be in his arms. Kiss him and so much more. However, that wasn't reality. They were not dating each other. This was dinner. When they left here, she would go home to her cold bed. *Cold and empty. Thanks, Shaun, for making me want what I can't have.*

She pulled her hand back. This wasn't a date, yet he was beginning to act as though it was. If she misunderstood, this would be a good time for him to let her know. "Shaun, I thought you wanted to talk about autism."

"I do, but that doesn't mean I don't want to talk about other things. Like you for instance."

I'm not that interesting. And you probably won't like me if you knew me. She needed to get back on the topic she thought they were there to discuss. "I didn't notice any company match programs in place."

"Excuse me?" Shaun looked puzzled.

"You know. A company match program where employees can donate to a non-profit organization and the company matches their donation. If you'd like, I can prepare a presentation for you to review next week on how it would work."

"Morgan, I would love to hear about it, but not tonight. Prepare whatever you'd like, but we're not talking work. Right now it's about you and me."

Her heart skipped not just one beat but several. There was no way she heard correctly. Did she miss something? She didn't remember there being a Shaun and Morgan. *Okay, we shared a kiss. A very hot kiss that haunts my every thought.* She wanted it to be true, that he might honestly want something more with her. *But I'm a package deal. He's trying, but he's not ready. He has no idea what type of commitment it is. He may want to hear and learn now, but there is no way he'd want that forever. And I don't need someone to come into our lives for a week or two. It's not fair to me and most definitely not to Tyler.* She needed to make him understand. But how, when she had no clue what was going on between them. She was even battling herself, and she couldn't afford to let her desires win.

"And Tyler," Morgan added in a flat tone.

He smiled and nodded. "And Tyler."

Stop smiling. Stop agreeing. You're not making this any easier. Don't you get it? I don't want to like you. It will only make it hurt later.

"Tell me about yourself, Morgan."

"I'm an only child. I have a small apartment above my parents. I have a nine-year-old son."

He laughed. "Okay, and you also work at Poly-Shyn in HR. Is there anything else you would like to tell me that I already know?"

She blushed and shook her head. There was no way she was going to ask him what he wanted to know because that would give him the power. "I went to Boston University?"

"I know. You graduated with a 4.0 GPA."

She was shocked. "How do you know that?" *Was he having me investigated?*

Shaun smiled. "Your mother enjoyed bragging about all your achievements."

"I hope she didn't pull out the photo album too."

"I'll have to ask about that next time." He winked at her teasingly. Yet, she didn't doubt for a minute he would ask. And knowing her mother, she'd have him sitting there for hours going over each picture.

"Don't you dare." Morgan laughed. She was enjoying herself. It shouldn't surprise her. He'd taken her to a fine restaurant, but it wasn't the food that was making the night. It was his company. He was charming and handsome as hell. But he also made her laugh, and she liked that most of all.

"So you seem to have already gotten the jump on me, thanks to my mother. Why don't you tell me about you?"

"I grew up in the Boston area, and I have four brothers and a sister."

Yes, Zoey, the one you led me to believe was a girlfriend. I still have no idea why you did that. "I have met Dean and Zoey." Morgan winked at him this time to let him know she hadn't forgotten their first meeting. "If I didn't know you three were siblings, I never would've guessed it. All three of you look so different."

"I've heard that all my life. We have a few similar traits, but that's all."

You want to know about me, but it's like pulling teeth to get you to talk about yourself. What gives? She wasn't going to give up so easily. But asking deeply personal questions wasn't her thing, so she kept it light. "Where do you fall in line?"

"Brice is the oldest. He's married to Lena, and they have a son, Nicholas, and are expecting their second child anytime. Then there's Logan, Alex, Zoey, me, and then the youngest, Dean, who is marrying Tessa, your boss."

"Wow! I would've loved to have grown up in a large family like that, and with the family growing, it must make the holidays even more special."

"Things are changing."

That's not saying much. Maybe they're not close. But one of six, you can't fight with them all, can you? "What about your parents?"

She saw his eyes darken, and his light and easygoing mood disappeared. Morgan had tried to stay on things that, for most people, were easy topics. The look said it was as bad as if he'd wanted to talk about Tyler's father. *No more questions from me unless it's to ask about the weather.*

Morgan thought he'd change the subject as she would've, but instead, he answered, though reluctantly and briefly.

"My father passed away last year, and I never knew my mother."

How could I have forgotten? It was all over the news; they'd had a private funeral. The late Mr. Henderson was one of the most powerful men in the US. Stupid Morgan. Real insensitive.

Morgan reached across the table and covered his hand with hers. "I'm sorry."

He lifted his eyes to meet hers, and she saw no pain as she would have expected, but they were filled with anger. At first, she thought it was at her. Yet, when he spoke, she realized it was deep-rooted pain that was speaking. She understood such things as she carried some herself.

"Don't be. He was far from pleasant, and he's not missed. Not by his family or anyone who knew him."

She was lucky to have both her parents and loved them both very much. Shaun's cold remark about his father shocked her. She thought he'd grown up in a home that most people envied. But his words said otherwise. *All the money in the world can't buy a loving home or happiness.* Her heart hurt for him. He might act as though the pain was in the past, but she saw differently. It was a wound running very deep and not a topic for tonight. *Maybe never. Some things aren't meant to be shared.*

His hand beneath hers was tense. Slowly she began to pull her hand from his, but he grabbed her fingers and held them to his.

"That probably sounded . . . horrible coming from one of his children. Actually, it is. But the dynamic of our family is nothing like you've seen before. It's much better with him out of the picture. If you knew him, you'd understand. Consider yourself lucky to have never met him."

As she looked into his eyes, she could tell that, even as he spoke, he was still holding back. She'd heard stories of abuse, and could only imagine how bad it must've been to affect someone as strong as Shaun.

"Let's just say that you're providing Tyler a much

better home and childhood than any of us ever knew. And you agreeing to come out with me tonight, even when you don't want to be here, only proves that more. You're not here for me or for yourself. You just wanted to explain what is best for Tyler so my entering his life will have a positive effect."

She was here for Tyler, but not just him. "You're wrong, Shaun."

"Am I?"

"Yes. Tyler is the most important person in my life, and I will do anything to protect him, but if I didn't want to be here with you right now, I wouldn't be."

She said it. Admitted to herself and him that . . . she enjoyed his company. Not in so many words, but she was sure she'd made her point.

He lifted her fingers to his lips and kissed them gently. "Let's get out of here."

HE DIDN'T LET go of her hand as they left the restaurant. Shaun wanted nothing but to feel more of her, all of her tonight. When he asked her to dinner, he never expected to talk about himself. Many women had been in his life, and not once did he share a thing with them, nor did he care about their life. Morgan was different. He knew the moment he set eyes on her a couple of weeks ago.

Sitting in the limo, the connection they had in the restaurant was fading. Strange because normally this is where he'd make his move and finish it at a hotel. Although his cock was hungry for her, something in him held back. *She deserves more than a cheap affair. What else can I give her? I'm not the serious relationship kind. And Morgan is exactly that. Serious.*

He sat still holding her hand as he pondered the issue. *Take her home, or take her to my bed?* Out of the corner of his eye, he saw her looking out the window as though in deep thought. *Maybe you're thinking the same thing. What should we do? What shouldn't we do?*

It was close to one in the morning, and he was far from ready for this night to end. Her place was off limits, and he could tell she wasn't ready for his. As they got closer to her house, they approached what looked like a local park. Shaun asked the driver to turn in.

"What are we doing here?"

"It's a lovely night. How about a walk?" *I must be losing my mind. I don't think I've ever walked in a park or played in a park. What the hell am I doing here?*

"You want to walk here? Are you sure it's safe?" Morgan looked out the window into the darkness then back to him.

I'm really not thinking this through at all. Can it get any less romantic than bringing a girl to a park and possibly running into a drug deal or some teenagers doing it on a swing? "No. This is not where I want to take you, Morgan." He reached around her pulling her close to him. "But I figured the park was safer than my apartment. For you at least."

Her eyes widened as though she didn't know how to take his statement. Then she relaxed in his arms and said,

"How about a walk around my block where we *both* can be safe?"

Shaun liked that she wasn't shocked or afraid of him in any way. *A woman who knows what she wants. I like that. Of course, I'd have liked it better if you wanted to come home with me.*

"Your block it is."

Walking hand in hand around the block made him feel like a teenager who had yet to experience the pleasures of a woman. But he found he enjoyed her company more than he'd expected. *More than I wanted.*

"How long have you lived here?"

"All my life, almost. I lived on campus when I went to college and had an apartment for a few years after that. Then after—"

He could tell she was so close to saying it. *Tell me about Walter. I want to hear you say it. It's the only way to move forward, to deal with the past.*

If only he took his own advice. He'd tried to bury all the abuse and neglect from his childhood. *Who am I kidding? It didn't end when I turned eighteen. It only changed and only stopped the day his father had a massive heart attack. If he were alive today, he'd probably still remind us of what pieces of shit we all are.*

He wasn't going to push her. No different than he didn't want to be pushed. *Anyone who tried found themselves in a very uncomfortable position.*

"I can see why you'd want to raise Tyler here. It's . . . nice."

"That's very kind to say, but I can picture what it looked like where you grew up. I'm sure you didn't play in a neighborhood like this."

"You're right. I didn't. Playing wasn't part of our regiment."

She stopped walking and looked up at him. Her beautiful honey brown eyes were searching his, hoping that he was joking. Sadly he was not. If it wasn't for the short intervals they were allowed to hang out with the Barrington family, they never would've been away from home except for school.

"We had a family we were allowed to visit from time to time. I'm sure it was because my father wanted or needed something from the Barringtons, but we didn't care. Going there and learning about what normal, loving families do was both a blessing and a curse."

Morgan touched his arm as she spoke to him. *Do you know what you do to me when you touch me like that? It makes me want to carry you back to the limo and touch you right back. From head to toe.*

"Why?"

"It showed us what a real family was like. One where people sat and spoke to each other at a dinner table. They have always treated us like family. Sophie, their mother, still sends each of us a birthday card every year. She's an amazing woman."

I can't help but wonder if our mother had been a part of our lives, would we have had a home life like the Barringtons? Probably not, because our father was still an asshole.

No matter how good a woman she was, he would've ruined her, just like everything he touched.

"Family comes in many forms."

"Coming from the woman who was born into a loving family."

"Yes, I was. One that knew they couldn't give me what I would need. So they put me up for adoption and Elisabeth and Loras have loved me as their own ever since."

What the hell, Bennett? Anything else you forget to tell me? As they walked up the steps onto her porch, he said, "I didn't know you were adopted."

"There's a lot you don't know, Shaun."

Shaun wrapped an arm around Morgan's waist and drew her up into his embrace. "I look forward to getting to know all there is to know. But for tonight I'll settle for a kiss."

He bent and kissed her so gently it was almost painful. He needed her. Wanted to rip her clothes off and kiss every inch of her soft sweet flesh. That would fulfill one need only. With Morgan, there was something more he wanted. He wasn't exactly sure what that was, but until he figured it out he was going to take it slow.

Just as he convinced himself to go slow, her arms wrapped around his neck and pulled him closer to her. Her mouth opened, and her delicious tongue traced his lips and slid inside. *Fuck slow.*

His arms tightened around her, pressing her breast firmly against his chest. Shaun took her tongue into his mouth, sucking it as it entwined with his. His free hand ran down her back and cupped her well-rounded ass. She moaned into his mouth, and his cock danced in response. *God, woman, I want you.*

As things heated up, an annoying sound interrupted the mood. There was a small dog barking from somewhere in front of the house. He released her slightly and out of the slit of his eye he saw an older woman walking her dog. *Who the hell walks a dog at two in the morning?* He lifted his head and held her gently against him. *And what grown-ass man gets caught necking on a porch by a neighbor? Really! Thirty-one and making out on the porch. What are you doing to me, Morgan? Never mind me trying to get to know you better. I think I better start figuring out who I am.*

Turning his attention back to Morgan he asked, "Should I come by at ten?"

She nodded. "I can't make any promises on how Tyler will react, but if you're willing to try at the pace he needs, then so am I."

Shaun walked back to the waiting limo. Nothing about tonight seemed like the usual him. Like Morgan, he couldn't make any promises. He could only take it day by day. *And today I promised to go slow. But tomorrow is another day.*

Chapter Eleven

"I CAN'T BELIEVE I agreed to this, Mom. So much can go wrong."

"And so much can go right. I already let Tyler get familiar with the bike; he seems to be in love with it, I think it's all that chrome. And besides, it's the same color as the two-seater. It's like Shaun understood not to change things too much. I really like him, Morgan."

Mom, aren't you supposed to see my side of this? She looked at the clock. It was almost ten, and it was time to have Tyler get his water bottle ready.

It only took one call to wake him this morning, and he was by her side, sneakers on and tied. *Now this is a good way to start the day. I hope it continues when Shaun gets here.*

There was no holding Tyler back. He knew what time it was, and he wanted outside. If she tried to stop him and tell him to wait, he would become agitated and take his sneakers back off, and she knew the bike ride would be off the list for the day.

Shaun hadn't shown up yet, so she assumed he might

have changed his mind after the major information dump she gave him. It wouldn't surprise her if he had second thoughts about whether he wanted to get to know them better. Heck, she'd had second, third, and fourth thoughts all morning. If she weren't equally scared of calling him and backing out, she would've done so earlier.

It was now a few minutes past ten. Tyler was becoming anxious. *I can't wait any longer.* She went outside with her mom and Tyler by her side. To her disappointment, the limo was nowhere in sight. *He's not coming.* As they descended the porch steps she saw her dad in the driveway speaking to someone. A smile lit up her face as she noticed it was Shaun, standing there dressed in a pair of jean shorts and a T-shirt. *Holy shit! That man looks good enough to . . . it's a good thing I'm riding in front or I wouldn't be able to keep my eyes off him.*

Shaking her head to clear her thoughts, she looked again to see if the limo was down the street, but she couldn't locate it. Then she saw a Jeep Wrangler with a bike rack on the back. She pointed in that direction. *Yours?*

He nodded and said, "I thought I would bring my bike in case the three-seater didn't work out today."

Oh, my God. Can this man get any more thoughtful? Please don't become irresistible. I can't afford to fall for you.

Loras walked over with Shaun to meet up with them. He stopped to give Elisabeth a kiss on the cheek then Tyler a playful tussle of the hair.

"Hi, Dad. I didn't think you would make it back home so soon."

"We got the water main repaired quicker than any of us thought. Guess no one wanted to spend their Saturday digging a new trench and laying pipe." Loras's clothes were still wet and covered in mud from whichever water main he'd been working on.

"Good, now you'll be here to see how Tyler likes the bike set up," Elisabeth said cheerfully.

"I was telling Shaun about the first time you took Tyler out on that bike. He never wanted to come back."

"That might be a bit of an exaggeration, but he sure was thrilled," Elisabeth commented.

Shaun replied, "I'm sure he'll let us know what he thinks about the new bike when he's ready."

Morgan could've hugged him right then and there. *He really was listening to me last night. This wasn't a bullshit story just to see if he could get in my pants. Damn I like him. I don't want to, but I like him.*

Tyler ran over to where the helmets were hung, put on his, then ran to the side of the garage where the bikes were stored. At first, they thought he'd go to the two-seater and say "up" as usual, but he stopped at the new bike Shaun had bought. He didn't climb on, but he didn't walk away. He stood staring at it.

Morgan walked over and asked, "Do you like this bike? It has three seats. One for Mommy. And the middle one for Tyler, and that one in the back is for our friend, Shaun."

Tyler stood just looking. Not moving and not showing any emotional reaction one way or another.

"Would you like to take the new bike out for a ride today so Shaun can come out and play too?"

He nodded.

"Use your words, Tyler. Do you want the new bike or the old bike?"

"New bike."

He was getting excited and wanted to get going. His hands started flying in front of him, and Morgan knew to get him on now, or they might lose the moment. She quickly pulled her helmet on and tossed a spare one to Shaun.

"We have to move fast." She walked Tyler to the seat in the middle and helped him on while Shaun held the bike steady, then climbed onto the front seat. Shaun took up the rear. "Is everyone ready?"

"Yes," Shaun answered.

"New bike. New bike," Tyler shouted as they all started pedaling down the driveway and onto the quiet street. It was nice to have a neighborhood where you could ride without many worries for speeding cars. It was a place where everyone watched out for each other.

As they passed by the postman, he waved and said, "Hello, Tyler."

Tyler replied, "New bike. New bike."

This was the same scene for each person they passed. Again and again the same two words. Morgan could picture Shaun rolling his eyes and wishing he was anywhere but on this bike with them.

She wished she could stop and explain to Shaun that Tyler was only repeating the words because of his excitement with the bike. Some days it was repeating a show he watched word for word. It didn't even matter if it was in English. He said it verbatim, never missing a thing. But what she enjoyed most was listening to him sing after listening to a song played on the radio. *You're one talented young man. Mommy wishes she had your singing voice. Mine makes the neighbor's dog howl.*

Morgan had taken the front seat as they had a certain path they followed. It took them almost an hour, and that was more than enough time. It provided a great excursion as well as keeping Tyler away from his IPad for a while.

Before she knew it, they were pulling back into the driveway. As soon as the bike stopped, Tyler jumped off, threw his helmet on the ground, and ran to the house. He knew it was snack time, and nothing was going to get in his way.

"Is everything okay?" Shaun asked from the back seat.

More than okay. That was perfect. "Yes. He knows my mother is waiting inside with something good to eat."

Shaun bent down and grabbed Tyler's helmet from the ground and hung it on the wall in the garage, then walked over and reached to take hers as well. She smiled as she handed it to him. It was a small gesture, but if felt nice to have someone, besides her parents, help her in any way. *Some days it's the little things that matter most.*

Each week she relished Tyler's bike riding time, but this week wasn't going to be forgotten. She had her parents there as back up all the time, but for the most part, it was just the two of them together. It would be a lie if she said she'd never dreamed of having someone in their lives, but she had never envisioned it coming true. It scared her to death, allowing herself to desire it again. Once the want was there, then the disappointment was sure to follow next. Shaun was proving himself to be so much more than she'd given him credit for. *Maybe more than he even realized by the look on his face.*

He was relaxed and smiling. It was the first time she'd seen him look so comfortable. Normally he was so darn serious as though his mind was running a million miles an hour, but at this very moment, he looked like he didn't have a care in the world. *You should try recreational relaxation more often.*

"Shaun, I want to thank you for today. When I saw the bike here yesterday I was so upset, but I see now that I was wrong."

He arched a brow. "Why did it upset you?"

Because you are doing what his father never has, and it hurts like hell. "Because you did it without even asking me first. I guess I'm used to being in control, and you'd taken that away from me."

"It's just a bike, Morgan. Trust me, you are and always have been in control."

Oh, I don't agree with that statement. If I were, I

wouldn't be a single mother right now. She did find it endearing that he saw her as a strong woman whether it was true or not.

"Would you like to come inside and have something cold to drink?"

"I have a few things I need to attend to. Maybe next time."

Will there be a next time? Are you planning on making this a habit? Don't start something that you can't finish. Remember what I said, Tyler works best with a routine. If you come around here too often, you will become part of it.

"Thanks again for coming. I can't believe how much Tyler liked his—"

"New bike." They said the words in unison and both laughed.

"I think we might hear those words in our sleep tonight." Morgan laughed.

"By the tenth time, I don't think I heard it anymore. It was like my brain had changed the frequency and blocked it from entering my ears," Shaun said, laughing softly.

"Wow! I'm very impressed." *Maybe more shocked. I thought you'd be running for the hills.*

"Why?"

"Normally you need to be a parent to acquire such super powers," Morgan teased him.

She saw him tense slightly at the word parent. *Got to watch what I say. He is far from interested in having a steady girl, never mind being a father.*

Morgan was angry with herself for letting the thought enter her mind. If Tyler's own father didn't want him, thought it was too much of a burden, then why would someone else who is even more successful want to take on that responsibility? *He wouldn't.*

"Shaun, thanks again, but I better get inside, and you said you had things you needed to do. I'll see you in the office on Monday."

She turned and started walking to the house. Each step was pulling at her, making her feel physically ill. It was as though she was putting the gap between them on purpose. A defensive move to protect her heart. Morgan was excellent at it. It just came with one price. *Being alone.*

SHAUN RESISTED REACHING out to her when she walked back to the house. Everything in him wanted to pull her into his arms and finish what they had started last night. But the rest of the day was time for her to spend with her family. Besides, he had some phone calls to make and those calls required privacy.

He didn't even bother to change when he headed to the office. He pulled up in front of the building and the security guard came out shouting, "You can't park here."

His face changed once he realized who he was barking at.

"Sorry, Mr. Henderson. I didn't realize that was you. New . . . vehicle?"

Shaun ignored the question, and the guard knew better than push further. He tossed the keys to him and said, "I'll call when I'm ready to leave." They didn't have valet parking, but today they did.

The guard looked at the keys, then back to the Jeep. "Yes, sir."

The guard wasn't the only one stunned by the Jeep. It'd been a spur of the moment purchase as he drove by the lot early this morning. That had never been the way he functioned. Everything he did was thought through thoroughly and calculated to optimize the outcome. Spontaneity was so out of character for him.

As a kid, he'd always wanted a Wrangler. To him, it represented freedom. The ability to go anywhere he wanted. He could own any car he wanted, but chose not to. He always had the limo pick him up and drop him off. It was convenient, and that's how he liked his life. Now he owned a Jeep and had no idea what he was going to do with it. *Maybe someday I'll do that off-road camping that appealed to me as a kid.* He laughed as he got off the elevator and made his way to his office. *What the hell am I thinking? I don't even like to sleep on a couch.*

He saw a light on in Dean's office, so he stopped there first. "Shouldn't you be home with Tessa?"

"Glad you're here. I wanted to bounce an idea off you."

Shaun sat on the couch and put his feet up on the coffee table. "What's up?"

Dean looked at him. "Maybe I should be asking you that first. I can't remember the last time I saw you dressed like that. Okay, I don't think I've ever seen you dressed like that. Are all your suits at the cleaners?"

"You don't know me as well as you think you do." The sad truth was Dean did. That's why he knew this was so damn unusual for him. *Fuck. I don't like anyone being able to read me so well. Not even family.*

"Whatever you say." Dean sat there grinning.

"You wanted to talk to me about something, so talk."

Dean had files scattered all over his desk. "I want to talk about Morgan."

The one person I don't want to talk about with you. "Business?"

"Is there more than that to discuss?"

"Don't fuck with me today, Dean. I've got a lot on my mind right now. So say what you need to and let me get busy handling my own shit." Shaun wasn't as frustrated with Dean as he was with himself. He was off his game, and that needed to change. There was something he needed to finish first, then he could put his concentration back where it belonged. *On work.*

Dean didn't pursue it. "I've been looking over the contract that Morgan altered. I'll tell you, we know our shit, but this woman is fucking amazing. The way she worded things brought this deal to an entirely new level. I need her."

"What the hell does that mean?"

"Easy brother, I'm still talking business here. But I'm telling you she's good, and Poly-Shyn needs her. Damn, the entire family could benefit from her skills. I just don't know if we can trust her after what went down at WS & Son."

"You can trust her. I'm not sure she's interested in that type of work any longer, but you can ask."

"I'm glad you think you can trust her, but your judgment might be clouded at the moment."

"And what is it you think I'm not seeing?" Shaun was pissed that Dean could question Morgan's integrity. *Damn. She's a better person than any Henderson ever will be. We've got no right to question anything.*

"Rumor has it she got fired for intentionally screwing up a contract on a major deal they were working on."

"And you got your information where?"

"Before I offered her a job heading up our contract division I wanted to hear what went down from the owner himself. My gut still said something was off even though Bennett didn't seem to find anything. Apparently, I was right."

Dean, you couldn't be more wrong. But why the hell would Sapp slam her like that? What did he have to gain? She's out of their lives. Wasn't that enough? Was he out to crush her? His chest was pounding with fury. If that was his rationale for slandering her name, then he was going to find out firsthand what it felt like to have his balls delivered to him on a platter. *I think it's time for Walter and me to have a chat.*

Shaun got up, his fisted hands wanting to make contact with something to release the anger within him. Dean was watching him closely but said nothing.

"Don't take any action yet. Just take my word, Dean. You can trust her, and that's all you need to know."

He walked out of Dean's office and entered his. He slammed the door behind him. As he sat at his desk, he ran his fingers through his hair. *Walter, you think you wish you'd never heard her name now, wait until you hear mine.*

Shaun pulled his cell out and dialed Bennett.

"I've got a job for you."

"More digging?"

Maybe a grave. "Security."

"Who did you piss off?"

No one yet. "Not for me; it's for Morgan and Tyler."

"Shaun, I know there is no reason she would need any protection, so I have to assume there is one coming."

Damn, you're good. "Possibly. I can't be there to watch them, so I need your men to. Nothing better happen to them. Do you hear me?"

"We're good at what we do, but I need to know who we're protecting her from."

"Walter is still fucking with them. I'm going to make him see what a huge mistake that is."

"And you'll be doing that how exactly?"

"Don't worry. I'm not going to kill him. Just financially crush the bastard and his father. When I'm done with them, they'll regret everything they said or did to those two."

Bennett was quiet for a minute then said, "I'll handle my end. Keep me in the loop on the status, and we'll up the level if needed."

"I don't care what it costs, Bennett. I need them safe."

"Teach that prick a lesson about how to treat women and children, and I'll do this one pro-bono."

"Maybe you're not the asshole I thought you were."

"Don't count on it. I take it Morgan knows nothing about what's going on, correct?"

"No one does and no one can."

"Nice and clean. Good luck."

Shaun ended the call. Luck wasn't something he used in business. If there was a risk, he never took it. What he had in store for WS & Son was costly, but it was going to be 100% effective.

He scrolled through his phone and found the number of a family friend who he thought might want in on something like this. Even though he was going after Walter, a tag-team effort was going to make it impossible for them to recover.

"Davis here."

"Trent. I'm in need of some assistance."

"You've never come to me before. What's so big that you need me now?"

Shaun gave him the details regarding Sapp's company.

"I need you to use your contacts to shut down any deal on the table for them. Any contracts that are pending. Any financial backing they have. You name it, shut it down."

"Shaun, I don't work like that any longer. I'm a family man now, remember?"

"Trent, this piece of shit needs to pay."

"I get that. But what I don't know is why?"

Because he's hurting people I care about. Shaun had no idea when he started caring. He never allowed himself to get close enough to anyone to care about them. Up until a few weeks ago, he would've said someone was crazy for taking something like this so damn personal. But all he could hear was Tyler's voice say *new bike* and Morgan's warm, loving eyes, and he knew he would do anything to protect them. Besides, he didn't start this; he was just the one who was going to finish it. There was no reason for Morgan to ever know. *Probably better she doesn't.*

Shaun explained the history behind what happened between Morgan and Walter. The details of how he'd rejected them because he considered his son less than perfect.

"The man has money and prestige. I want both taken from him. I want him to question if he can afford to order from the dollar menu at a fast-food drive-thru. His days of looking down on people who are in need are over. Time for him to be the one in need."

"I'm no knight in shining armor, but this guy's a real piece of work."

"That's putting it nicely, Trent. So are you in?"

"I'm in. A project like this will take a few weeks to chip slowly away at, so it doesn't raise a red flag right away, but if we line it up between my contacts and both of us, it is very doable."

"Excellent. One last thing. No one can know, including my family, about Morgan's history with the Sapp family. I need her left out of everything."

"You've got to protect the ones you love," Trent said before he hung up.

This has nothing to do with love. I'm just doing what's right.

Chapter Twelve

I T WAS ALREADY Thursday, and he wanted to call her, see her again. The days seemed to run together between keeping up with his own business, covering HR for Poly-Shyn, and spending quite a few hours working with Trent to make sure everything was lining up to explode at just the right time. *Right this second couldn't be soon enough for me, but I want it done correctly, not quickly. I want them to feel the pain as it all starts slipping through their cold-hearted, money-hungry hands. I want to watch them scramble and find no one there with a lifeline. Imagining them out on the curb, just like they basically did to their own flesh and blood, brings me great satisfaction.*

As he looked back at his last few hours of work, it was amazing and scary to see how many contacts he and Trent held power over. People who might not want to cut their ties with WS & Son but would because they feared they would be targeted next. He knew Trent's reputation. Even though he said he didn't play hardball any longer, just the mention of his name was enough to get a conversation flowing that might've otherwise ended. When he started making calls, people noticed Dean wasn't the only shark in the Henderson family. *Maybe I have more of my father in me than I want to admit. But at times like this, it comes in handy.*

When he passed Morgan earlier in the hallway, she said she was on her way to Dean's office. The next time she was with a coworker, and they were running to a meeting. It looked like the only way he was going to get to spend time with her was to schedule something himself. Just having her come to his office so he could kiss and touch her was not going to get the response he was looking for. He needed a valid reason. One she'd be enthusiastic about, but what the hell could that be?

Yes! He picked up his office phone and dialed her extension.

"HR, this is Morgan."

Her sweet voice was like nails running across his chest. Instantly he wanted her. "Do you have an opening on your calendar to discuss the company match program?" He'd already accessed her schedule and knew she didn't.

"Today and tomorrow aren't good. Can we schedule another time?"

"Yes, we can. I'll pick you up tonight at eight."

"Wait. What?"

"We'll have dinner, and you can present the program to me."

"Yes, but I can do that much easier in the office."

But it's not as fun. "You said this program would be

great for the non-profit agencies. I'm sure you can clear one night for me so we can get this ball rolling. No time like the present."

All was quiet on her end of the phone. He knew she was weighing her options. She was a thinker, and that was one more thing he liked about her. *Not clinging and ready to jump in my bed. But God, I want you there.*

"Tyler goes to bed at eight thirty. I would prefer to be home for that. Would nine be too late?"

"I'll pick you up then."

He leaned back in his leather chair with his arms resting behind his head. *That was easier than I thought. I wonder if she really believes I only want to talk business. There's no way she's that naïve.*

"I SHOULD'VE TOLD him no."

Elisabeth laughed. "You know you want to go. Don't even try pretending otherwise. You're a beautiful young woman and need to get out. And goodness knows that man is into you. The way he looks at you when you're not watching makes me think of the way Loras looked at me when we were dating."

"Oh, Mom, you know Dad still looks at you that way. Even after forty years."

Her mother blushed. "Morgan, that's what I want for you. And I think you might've just found it. But you're going to need to put some effort into this. If you keep pushing him away, one day he won't come back. But don't do anything you don't want to do. If you want to spend the night with him, then do it. If you don't, tell him so."

"Don't you try giving me the sex talk at this age. I think I will pee myself if you do." Morgan was trying to keep her laughter down as not to wake Tyler.

"Oh, don't act like you don't need one. I mean you have been cooped up in this house for six years. I don't think I cou—"

"Don't say it. I don't want to know." Morgan covered her ears.

She loved the relationship she had with her mother. But no matter how close they were she didn't want to hear the personal details of her love life. *What kid does?*

"Okay, I won't say it if you go change that outfit and put on your white dress, please."

"This is not a date. We are meeting to talk about a program I would like to initiate."

"Oh, my. How can someone so smart be so dense?"

"Mother! That's not very nice."

Elisabeth laughed. "No, but it's true. Will you open your eyes? This man is not picking you up at nine to talk business. Trust me. He could've had you email the information to review at his leisure."

Morgan thought about it. *Yeah, why make me come out just to discuss what really will only take ten minutes?* "This is crazy. Why waste time like this? He knows we're both very busy. If he wanted a date, why didn't he just ask for a date?"

"Because it *is a date!*" Elisabeth said, her voice louder

than either of them wanted.

"Okay," Morgan whispered. "It's a date."

"Good. Now get out of those business clothes and wear something . . . sexy. Show him you appreciate his attention."

"Mom, you're so old school."

"And you, dear girl, are so out of practice. I already told your father I am spending the night up here with Tyler, so don't worry if for some reason you don't make it home till morning."

What mother tells her child to stay out all night? Isn't she supposed to lecture me about getting my priorities straight? Of course, she wasn't going to waste any time telling her that. She had ten minutes to change and fix her makeup. *Not because you're right, but I'll feel better in this cute outfit.*

It was a lovely night, so she had the windows open. Her pulse quickened as she heard a car door shut. *And now I find out. Business or date.* She moved the curtain and peeked through the blinds, wanting to see him. As she watched him open the front gate and head toward the porch, she saw he was carrying flowers. *Date.*

Morgan was glad she listened to her mother. Not only did she change out of her stuffy business suit, but she also changed her undergarments too. She wanted this to be more, but she wasn't going to allow herself to hope for it. The scars from previous rejections, though covered, were still there. It wasn't Walter rejecting her that hurt at all. They'd honestly only been together because it was convenient. There never was any passion or love between them. The scars she carried were from watching him dismiss their child. Morgan couldn't bear it if she let Shaun into her life, their life, and he eventually decided it'd been fun, but it was over.

He's not Walter. Shaun is amazing. He's shown me how good he is with Tyler. He's gentle, caring, and patient. He wouldn't . . . couldn't . . . hurt us like that. And although it petrified her to take a chance and open herself up to him, it hurt far more to deny what she felt. *I want to be with him. If he doesn't kiss me tonight, I think I'll die.*

She looked in the mirror one last time. *Tonight Morgan, don't hold back. Let him know what you want. Stop being afraid. What's the worst thing that can happen? He says no. Better to find out now than later.*

Morgan heard the light knock on the door. *He knows Tyler is sleeping. It's like it comes natural to him. How? He doesn't have children. I don't even know if he wants any. But I know he's great with them, or at least with Tyler.*

When she opened the door, he looked past her for a moment, as though confirming they were alone, then pulled her into his arms and kissed her. It was like fireworks exploding within her. How she missed and wanted him.

It was too brief, but anything more would've made it impossible for her to stand; her legs already threatened to give way. She could pretend it was because she'd eaten only a light meal earlier, but they both knew he had the power to make her melt. *And that's just with a kiss.*

"Are those for me?"

"For the babysitter."

"My mother?"

"Without her, we wouldn't be going out tonight."

"Don't be making my husband jealous," Elisabeth said as she came into the hallway and took the flowers from him. "They're beautiful. Thank you, Shaun. Now get out of here before Loras and I sneak out in that limo parked out front."

Morgan grabbed her purse and kissed her mother on the cheek. "Call me if you need me. I'll keep my cell phone on."

Shaun handed Elisabeth a card. "And here is mine. Call for anything."

Elisabeth took the card and said, "You never know when this may come in handy. But not to worry, it won't be tonight." She smiled and winked at Shaun.

Really, Mom, you're killing me here. "Bye, Mom." Morgan took Shaun's hand and led him out of the house before her mother could embarrass her any further. As they walked down the pathway, she said, "Sorry about that. She just—"

"Loves you."

Morgan nodded. "Yes, she does."

The driver opened the door, and they slipped inside. Shaun never let go of her hand. His fingers entwined with hers. She wasn't a petite wallflower, but her hand seemed so tiny compared to his large one. As his fingers slid over hers playfully, he asked, "What do you want to eat?"

What I'm hungry for, isn't on any menu. "I . . . I'm . . . what would you suggest?" She couldn't think straight. All she wanted was to be alone with him, not in a crowd where she'd need to keep her hands to herself. *Calm down. Let him take the lead. I can't be throwing myself at him. It's not . . . ladylike.*

"Going to my place with some takeout food and cold—"

"Beer."

He brought her hand to his lips and kissed it. "Yes, beer."

Mom, I'm so glad you talked me out of wearing that stuffy business suit and my granny panties. Morgan rested her head on his shoulder as they made their way to his house. She actually had no idea where he lived, but she could picture it, based on how he dressed: neat, orderly, and very masculine.

When they entered his penthouse suite, her guess was confirmed. But she noticed it was void of anything personal. Not one picture or trophy. It looked more like a model home than a lived-in home. There was no sign of the man she'd come to know. *Maybe in his bedroom. But I'm not about to ask.*

He still held her hand as he guided her inside. "We could eat here or out on the balcony."

"It's a lovely night. I say outside."

"Why don't you go out, and I'll get us some beer."

She did as he suggested. Once outside, she saw his

getaway. A piece of him. It was similar to her backyard but much classier. On one side there were lounge chairs and side tables. She could see he must spend a lot of time out there. Business magazines and books were near one of the chairs. She almost took a seat there, but she heard what sounded like running water. She went around a six-foot-high stone wall and saw a running waterfall with a statue of a half-naked Greek goddess holding a basin of water overflowing into a small endless swimming pool. You could sit on the edge of one side, but it looked like if you swam to the other side you would go right over the edge of the building. *Wow. Breathtaking. Beautiful. A glassed-in infinity pool! I'm glad I'm on this side.*

Morgan sat on the edge of the pool and let her thoughts wander to the possibilities of what lay ahead. It wasn't just a moment in time. Tonight would be the night she was letting go of some of her excess baggage, allowing herself to enjoy the closeness of being with a man she'd come to adore. *I'm a thirty-six-year-old mature woman; there's nothing wrong with being confident enough to say and do what I want. And tonight I want to be with Shaun in every way. I'm tired of being shut-off and feeling nothing. It stops tonight! Tomorrow is another day.* A refreshing cool breeze came by and blew a stray leaf into the water not far from her, snapping her out of her musings. She leaned over to pluck it from the otherwise pristine pool.

"There you are."

Shaun's husky voice startled her. As she tried to sit

back up, she lost her balance. The harder she tried to regain it, the farther she slipped toward the water. With a not so subtle splash, she found herself fully submerged. She tried to stand, but found it was not as shallow as she'd first thought. Normally she'd enjoy a late night swim, but not clothed in her vintage white dress.

When she surfaced she had lost her bearings. *Damn. I'm at the other edge. Shit. Swim away. Don't think about it. It's not going to break. You're not going to fall over the edge of a thirty story building.*

Until then she never realized she had a fear of heights. *Maybe just a fear of falling from them.* As she tried to calm her nerves, there was another splash and Shaun was right by her side still in his suit as well. *Does he think that I can't swim? I was on the swim team at BU.* When he pulled her to him, she lifted her arms to wrap them around his neck. *But you don't need to know about that yet because I like this much better.*

His arm pulled her close while he brought them both back to the edge of the pool. There she could tell his feet made contact with the bottom. Morgan could reach for the side and pull herself up, but no way was she releasing him. It had been too long since she'd felt his arms around her.

"Are you okay?" Shaun brushed the wet strands of hair from her face.

She nodded. "Thank you for jumping in after me. I hope you didn't ruin your suit."

"I don't care about the suit or your dress. You never

mentioned if you could swim and all I could think was—"

"Saving me?"

"I'd never let anything or anyone hurt you, Morgan."

His voice was softer than she'd ever heard it before. He wasn't flirting with her. It was a proclamation of what? His feelings? A commitment of some kind? Whatever it was, it touched her heart. She'd never before felt as safe as she did now in his arms.

"I know." There wasn't anything more to say.

"Come on. Let's get out of here before these clothes weigh us down."

He put his hands around her waist and in one motion lifted her out of the water and back onto the edge of the pool. Then he pulled himself out as well. Shaun swung his legs around to stand back on the ground. The water was running off his suit, and she heard his shoes slosh with each step. She chuckled at the sight.

"Find this funny, do you?"

"A bit, yes." Morgan loved teasing him. When she did his eyes sparkled and his jaw relaxed.

"Then you will love to know your pretty white dress is totally see-through when it's wet. Love your polka-dot bra and panties."

Morgan looked down to find it was true.

"I suggest we get out of these wet clothes and warm up by the fire."

There was enough heat flowing through her already; she didn't need a fire to warm her. All she needed was his touch. She reached behind her and unzipped her dress letting it fall at her bare feet. *I had shoes when I went into the pool. Hmm.*

Standing clothed only in her bra and thong, she met his smoldering gaze. "I believe you said *we.*"

She'd never in her life been so bold or suggestive. But with Shaun, she found herself taking chances she thought impossible. He brought out a flirtatious, carefree side she never knew she had.

He took off his jacket and tossed it on the ground—then his tie. He unbuttoned his shirt, and she so badly wanted to help him. He was taking too damn long and, by his expression, it was on purpose. Once his shirt was removed, he acted as though he was struggling with the belt buckle.

That's it! She stepped forward and her hands brushed his away. That buckle was coming off if she needed to bite through the leather. He said nothing as he watched her trembling hands finally free it. The button on his pants popped off as she tugged with a bit more force than she realized. *Oh, God. What's wrong with me?*

"I'm sorry."

His voice was deep and filled with need. "I don't care if you shred them. You're so damn beautiful, and if I don't touch you soon, I'm going to lose my mind."

Her pulse raced. She felt the same way. Never before had she wanted or needed anyone so much. "Please." It was the only word she could say.

Shaun finished undressing and stood naked in front of her. He was perfect. Every inch of him toned and solid. Reaching out, she ran her tiny hand up his chest. He brushed it away.

"I want to see all of you, Morgan." He slipped a finger under one bra strap and slid it off her shoulder, then the other. He pulled her close to him and reached behind her, finding the clasp and releasing it, letting it drop. Then he hooked each of his thumbs on the strings of the thong on her hips, and as he dropped to one knee, he slid it off her.

"Tell me what you want."

Morgan looked down at him as he knelt only inches away from her most private area. She felt no shame as she replied, "You, now."

Shaun groaned, rose, and swept her into his strong arms. Being near him broke down all her inhibitions. All she felt was an overwhelming need to touch and be touched.

She'd never felt fragile, but as he carried her into the house he made her feel like fine porcelain. Nothing he was doing was rushed, even though she could feel his pulse race and his obvious need press against her.

Shaun kicked open a door to what appeared to be his bedroom. It was exactly how she pictured it, solid like him. He laid her gently on the center of the king-sized bed yet didn't release her. His eyes swept over her hungrily as though he was trying to decide where to start. *I know a good place. I'm aching for your touch. I need you inside of me.*

His warm hand gently ran up the length of her leg,

over her hip, finally resting on her collarbone. She leaned into his touch with more yearning than she'd thought possible.

She reached out, wanting to run her hands all over his rock-hard body, but he brushed her hand away. "I want to take this slow and enjoy every inch of you, but if you touch me, it will be over before it even starts."

Morgan looked him over hungrily and felt his manhood move against her as though she'd physically touched him. Knowing how strongly he wanted her heightened her nearly out-of-control desire. She bit her lip and closed her eyes, trying to maintain even the slightest control.

He kissed her forehead, then trailed kisses down her cheekbone, over her, and to her neck. Raw need exploded within her. She heard the words *take it slow,* but the fire building within her center was screaming otherwise.

Shaun cupped one breast and plucked at her taut nipple. A shiver ran through her body, and she arched against him. His kisses continued to trail up her body until his fingers were replaced by his mouth. Once his lips came in contact with her nipple, her body began to twitch in unison with his. "Shaun." Her voice trembled with need. He ignored her pleas and continued to flick with his tongue, or nip with his teeth, and it only increased her desire. "Shaun," she pleaded, her voice barely a whisper now. *Oh, God, I can't wait. I need him now.*

"Patience, baby," Shaun said, his words muffled by

her flesh.

Her moans grew deeper as he rolled one nipple between his fingers and continued sucking the other. The need between her legs was almost unbearable. Her plea didn't fall on deaf ears as she opened her legs. "Please, Shaun, I need . . ."

He didn't deny her. He moved one hand from her breast and reached between her legs, finding her swollen clit with this thumb. Her back arched, and she opened more for him.

Slowly, he circled it, bringing her higher. As her body trembled, he repositioned himself so his mouth was now only inches away from her center, spreading her farther until he had full access. Her hands gripped the blanket as he slipped one finger inside her and pulled it back out. Then again and again.

Breathlessly, Morgan begged, "I want you. I can't . . ."

"You'll have me, but first I want to watch you come undone as you lose yourself, surrendering to my touches," he said as his finger entered her again, and he continued to circle her clit. She cried out in pleasure. It was more than she'd ever experienced. He was giving, not taking.

Faster and deeper he made love to her with his finger until her body jerked violently, and she lost herself in a powerful release.

"Yes! God, Shaun. Oh, yes!"

Before her body settled, he left her for a moment.

She heard him open the foil packet before returning to her. She needed more than his finger. She needed him deep inside her. She wanted to wrap herself around him and give him the pleasure he'd just given her.

He didn't enter her right away. Instead, he stroked her with the head of his shaft until she trembled. He slowly guided himself through her folds, then back to her clit. Her body, still so sensitive from the first climax, reignited for a second, quivering under his. "Shaun!"

As she released, Shaun plunged deep within her. Her body clenched tightly around him. He lay upon her as her body continued to rock.

Once she quieted, he began to move in her.

She looked up at him and saw desire burning deep within him. He couldn't wait any longer, and she knew it.

"Shaun, give me what I want. I want all of you." Her breathing was coming in short gasps.

"God, baby. You feel amazing," Shaun said, never taking his eyes off hers. Again and again, he buried himself deep inside. She pulled him down to her, and he captured her lips with his as their moans of pleasure blended together. They were not slow any longer. She could feel the raw need as he was losing control. Fast and furious, he entered again and again.

"Morgan. I can't—"

"Yes, Shaun. Give it to me. Let go."

It was as though the heavens opened up; a feeling like nothing before rocked them both. Her cries met with his deep growl as he released. He gripped her hips for one last deep thrust before collapsing into her waiting arms.

A single tear trickled down her cheek, and she brushed it away.

He lifted himself up to look at her. "Fuck. Did I hurt you?"

She shook her head. "Shaun, you could never hurt me."

What they shared was so much more than she'd ever imagined. She knew she was safe with him. And for the first time since becoming a mother, she knew her son was safe with someone besides her and her parents. *You've given me more tonight than you'll ever know. More than I can ever say.*

Chapter Thirteen

"T HAT WAS QUICK."

"Bennett, I told you, when the chain of events starts, people are going to notice quickly." At least people who give a shit about what happened with the Sapp family. He, on the other hand, never would've given them a second look. They had a very successful, growing business. But they would learn, compared to his family's company, their business was small and could be easily squashed.

Bennett took another gulp of coffee. "I have someone watching the house at all times. Did you want someone on the inside at Poly-Shyn as well?"

Shaun hadn't thought about that. His only concern had been for Morgan and Tyler. For as long as he could remember he'd only thought of his family's protection. *When did that change? Why did it?*

"It won't affect Poly-Shyn. If they look for a culprit, I'll make sure it's me they see."

Bennett arched his brow. "You're making yourself the target. What am I missing?"

"Nothing." *If I wanted you to know my plan, then I'd inform you. No one knows it all and no one will.*

"Shaun, I respect what you're doing for Morgan and Tyler, but I'll put a stop to it if you go too far." Bennett's face had no hint of backing down.

"And you think you can stop me?"

"Any day. You do your job well. But so do I. Don't forget that."

"You're not threatening me are you, Bennett?" It'd been a long time since anyone had the balls to speak to him like that. Shaun wanted to hate the guy, but the more he got to know him, the more he respected him.

"I don't deal with threats." Bennett's phone beeped.

Shaun watched as he checked the message. Whatever it was, it didn't make him happy. "Problems I should know about?"

"Zoey is at lunch with Morgan. I didn't realize they were friends."

Damn it, Zoey. This is no time to become buddies with Morgan. All it will mean is another person for Bennett to cover. "She's a very—"

"Beautiful woman."

"Don't even think it, Bennett. My sister is off limits. If I even think that you're—"

"I don't mix business with pleasure. And trust me, she would be a pleasure." Bennett laughed.

You're just fucking with me. It's a dangerous game, but I know you're not stupid enough to actually go after my sister. Hell no. Not that dumb.

175

"Is there anything else that concerns you at this time?"

"Tomorrow's bike ride is going to be tough without being noticed. It's a very tight neighborhood. My men are good but, there's no way they won't be noticed. If not by her, then one of her neighbors. Damn, every neighborhood should have a crime watch program like theirs."

If it were only that simple; they were used to the quiet, peaceful life. They watched each other, mainly for the sake of gossiping, but that is because no trouble had come to them. What would they do if it did? It would be too late. No matter what, he wanted to make sure there was someone close by at all times. If it couldn't be Bennett's team, then there was just one who could be there.

"Don't worry about it. I'll be there with them for the ride and possibly most of the weekend. I'll let you know if plans change."

He was the one who'd decided to push the issue with Walter, to make him crumble and fall. No harm should be sent Morgan's way, but he knew all too well not to trust a wounded animal, and that is what the Sapp family was going to feel like when he was done with them.

Even if there was no potential threat, Shaun wanted to be with them anyway. He truly enjoyed Morgan's company. He didn't want her to leave last night. Holding her in his arms, his bed felt like nothing he'd ever had before. The connection they shared scared him more than any threat from Walter. There were all these thoughts running through his head, and for once in his life, he couldn't organize them rationally. Even now his mind continued to wander back to her. He could understand if it was just her beautiful olive skin, but it wasn't. He was lost in her eyes, her smile, and her bubbly personality. She was the type of woman who made a man want to go home at night. *Too bad I'm not the type of man to appreciate such a gem.*

"You seem to be getting close to them. First rule of protection, don't ever let your feelings get in the way of your gut."

"I don't need you to tell me how to protect my—"

Bennett only smiled. "Exactly." He downed the remainder of his coffee and got up from the table. "I'm off to accidentally bump into your sister and Morgan for lunch. Wish me luck."

Shaun wanted to pop the guy in the face, but the truth was he knew Morgan and Zoey couldn't be in better hands. Bennett would never let anything happen to either of those ladies. *For now, I can stop worrying about her and concentrate on some sliding stocks.* He laughed slightly. *This is like shooting fish in a pail of water. I just can't miss.*

"THIS IS CRAZY. I'm just being paranoid. There is no one watching me. Why would there be?"

"Why don't you talk to Shaun about it? I'm sure he'd want to know. I know your father would want me to talk to him about something troubling me," Elisabeth said as she and Morgan cleared the table after dinner.

"What would you tell me?" Loras asked as he came back into the kitchen and grabbed a freshly baked chocolate chip cookie from the jar.

Morgan shot her mother a warning look, but it didn't stop her.

"Our daughter is worried that she is being watched."

Loras stopped mid-bite and looked at Morgan. "Are you serious?"

She shrugged. "I haven't seen anyone. It's just a feeling I've had for a few days. I've looked over my shoulder a million times and have seen no one. So it has to be my imagination."

"I don't like this."

"Dad, really. Mom is making this out to be more than it needs to be. You know Dora and her sister on the corner would be the first to notice anyone strange. I mean they practically sit on their porch with binoculars. Heck, maybe they're the ones watching me." Morgan laughed, trying to make the conversation light and normal even though she still wasn't convinced herself.

"I'm going to take a walk; I'll be back."

Her father was a stubborn man. There was no way to stop him once he had decided to do something. Offering to go with him would only mean getting a lecture on how she needs to be more careful. *I live such a boring life, any safer and I'll vanish into the background.*

But that was her life a few weeks ago. Now things had changed. Her days, which she could have predicted months in advance, now spun wildly at times. Maybe that was what she was feeling, all the changes. *Especially after last night with Shaun.*

Her body tingled all day from his loving touch. She'd had a few lovers before, but what she shared with Shaun last night didn't seem like sex. It was more intimate than anything she'd ever known. She'd told herself to enjoy it because she didn't know how long they were going to be together. But it went beyond enjoying herself. It was a connection she hadn't thought she would feel. Yes, she was flirting and bolder than she'd ever thought she could be, but there was an emotional part that overwhelmed her. Because of that she knew it was best not to spend the entire night at his home. Waking up in his bed was only going to make it more difficult to say goodbye later. She never was a casual affair type of woman. What made her think she was capable of it now? *And with a man like Shaun.*

"Earth to Morgan. Are you even listening to me anymore?"

Morgan blushed. "Sorry, Mom. I was thinking about . . ."

"Yeah, I know, Shaun."

"No."

Elisabeth laughed. "Honey, you let out a long sigh and said his name breathlessly."

Morgan slumped into the seat near her. "Oh, God. What have I done to myself?"

"I think you know. And it's a good thing. About

time. You can't live your life for Tyler only. You have to remember you're not just a mother; you're also a woman."

"You make it sound so simple, but what if he's not the type of man that can—?"

"Love someone like you? Or love someone like Tyler?" Her mother's voice was sharp for the first time in a long time.

She wanted to tell her mother she was wrong with those questions, but in fact, she'd nailed it. Those were the exact doubts she had. Shaun, even though he was here now, wasn't going to be here for the long haul. It's easy to go for a bike ride, but it was the day in and day out that made a difference. She wasn't going to ask her mother to watch Tyler so she could run off at night and play with Shaun. It wasn't fair to any of them. No matter how or what she felt last night, she wasn't going to let it become a habit with her.

I may be falling in love with Shaun, but that doesn't mean he feels anything close to that for me. I have to keep tight reins on my emotions, or I'm going to self-destruct when it comes to an end. And it will, eventually.

"You're right. I have to stop this before it gets out of hand."

"Or you can let the man in. He wants in, but you're either too stubborn or blind to see. Don't jump to conclusions. Shaun is making an effort, and you need to as well."

Morgan didn't want to open those lines of communication with him. It was only going to put him on the spot and make her uncomfortable. *Why do I need to hear it? I already know what the answer is going to be.*

Her phone vibrated. She pulled it out of her pocket. *Hmm. Were your ears burning, Shaun?*

"Hi."

"I was hoping to see you at work today, but I was tied up all day."

"I was as well. Was there something you needed?"

"Yes. You."

Morgan blushed, and her heart skipped a beat. *Don't make me want you more than I already do.* She couldn't answer him with her mother sitting there, staring at her.

"Anything besides that?"

"Yes, I just wanted to remind you I'll be there tomorrow for your ride. Ten a.m."

Reminder? I never knew you were coming again. "Okay. I'll see you in the morning then."

"Are you going to dream of me tonight?" Shaun's voice was soft and teasing, sending a warm feeling through her.

Why wouldn't I? I've been dreaming of you since the day I met you. Only now I know what I'm missing, and it's even more than I dreamt about. "We'll see."

She ended the call and turned to face her mother again. She was grinning from ear to ear. *Really. Nothing better to do than torture me?*

"I've got to get Tyler ready for bed. Good night, Mom."

Elisabeth laughter echoed through the room as she said, "Sweet dreams, Morgan."

Oh, God. She heard. Thanks Shaun for feeding into her hopes. She's not going to let me forget this one. But there is something so much bigger I know I'll never forget, and that is you.

Chapter Fourteen

"WE HAVE AN issue."

"With Morgan?" Shaun's voice filled with panic.

"Her father, Loras, knows we're watching the house, watching her."

"How the fuck did that happen?" Shaun wasn't ready for Morgan to know what was going on. If she found out, there was no telling what her reaction would be. *She should be happy that someone is dealing with that asshole. But probably not.*

"I guess Morgan said something to him, and he had all the plates of unknown vehicles run. When ours came up, he came knocking."

Shit. He was already on his way to her house for their bike ride. She hadn't called him, so was she waiting for him to get there before confronting him? "What did you tell him?"

"Times like this, you tell something close to the truth."

I like that saying. "And that was?"

"That you cared deeply about Morgan and Tyler and wanted a bit of security watching her. That you'd caught wind that the Sapp family wasn't doing as well as before, and you didn't want any of their issues coming down on Morgan."

Not bad. "What did he say?"

"That he'll discuss it with you while Morgan and Tyler go for the ride. It looks like dear ole dad wants to have a sit down with you, Shaun. Good luck."

Shaun didn't miss the sarcasm. But he couldn't sit with Loras because he needed to be on that bike, watching Morgan. There wasn't much time to develop a plan. He pulled in front of her house, and Loras was waiting by the gate. "Keep your guys alert. I might not be on the ride this morning."

"Roger that."

Shaun got out of the Jeep and walked right up to Loras. "I think we should talk."

"You took the words right out of my mouth, young man," Loras said, then called out, "Morgan."

She came out of the house. "Yes, Dad?"

"Shaun and I are going to get some coffee while you and Tyler take your ride."

He watched Morgan's eyes widen even before she looked at him puzzled. "Is there something either of you want to tell me?"

"No," they replied in unison.

Morgan put her hands on her hips and said, "I'm not a child."

"No, but you're still my daughter, and Shaun and I are going to sit down for a little man-to-man time. Your choice is to go on the bike ride with Tyler or stay in the house. We should be back within an hour."

"Loras, what are you up to?" Elisabeth asked, now standing by Morgan.

"Being a father," Loras replied and headed toward Shaun's Jeep. "You can drive."

He'd never encountered having to sit and explain himself to someone's parent. *Hell, I never explained myself to my own father.* "Where to?"

"I don't care. Just make it out of this neighborhood to a place we can talk privately."

Shaun started the Jeep but pulled out his cell phone and sent a quick text to Bennett, letting him know the new plan before driving off.

He wasn't familiar with the area, but came across a small breakfast place. "Is this okay?"

"Fine with me."

Shaun could hear the tenseness in Loras's voice. If the tables were turned, he probably would've demanded the answer right there on the front walk, never waiting for a private moment to speak.

The waitress came and took their order. Once they had their drinks Loras started the conversation.

"I had a chat with your friend, Bennett. Let's just say I am not accepting his answer to my question. So now I'm going to ask you, and you better have an explanation as to why you're having my daughter watched."

So many things came to mind. Tell the man it's none of his business and see what he does. He could make up a lie. "Morgan is not aware of what I am going to tell you."

"I figured that much. After you tell me, I'll decide if she needs to know."

He could respect that. "Fair enough. Let me start by saying that I care about your daughter very much."

"If I thought otherwise I wouldn't be sitting here with you."

He nodded. "This is about Tyler's father, Walter."

"What's that bastard up to now?" Loras's voice became louder than he expected and people around him turned and looked in their direction. He gave them a wave of apology and addressed Shaun again. "If he thinks after all this time he can walk back into their lives he has another thing coming."

"No, that's not the issue. He and his family are still as hateful as they were six years ago."

"Then what's going on?"

"They are slandering her name in the business industry. So I decided it was time to shut them up once and for all."

Loras had a look of concern. "And how do you plan on doing that?"

There are things you are better off not knowing. "By hitting him where it'll hurt him the most. His one true love."

"His wallet."

Exactly. "I've left Morgan out of this. They should

have no reason to link anything to her, but a cornered dog will bite, and I want them protected." He didn't care if he took the hit, but if anything happened to her, he'd never forgive himself.

"How far are you taking it?"

"All the way."

"Closing the company?"

Crushing it. "Yes."

"Shaun, I respect you want to defend her honor, but you need to think of all the employees who'll lose their jobs. What you're doing is going to have a chain reaction that affects innocent families. Morgan would never want to hurt another child to protect her own. That's not who she is."

He hadn't thought that far. There had only been one mission, and that was to make him pay for what he'd done to her and to Tyler. Technically it wasn't too late. He could contact Trent, and together they could put a halt to it, but then what did they gain? *Nothing.*

If I crush Walter and lose Morgan, is it worth it? She could go back to her life, and I go back to mine. Would that be so bad? I wasn't looking for anything serious to start, so cutting my ties would be the wisest choice. He downed his coffee and waved the waitress for a refill.

"I don't want him in her or Tyler's life ever again."

"That's hard. He is Tyler's father. There is such a thing as parental rights. He could walk back in anytime he wants to, and there is nothing any of us can do to change that, whether he has money or not."

187

Shit. How could I have forgotten that? Oh, because I'm not a parent. I don't know this shit. He ran his fingers through his hair. Frustration filled him, and he felt as though he was back to square one.

"Shaun, you might want to stop and think about why you're doing this before you continue. I know you said you care about Morgan, but your actions are . . . extreme. Something you'd expect from someone who loves a woman. Do you love her?"

Love? I don't know anything about such feelings. They've never been part of my life. "I like her . . . very much."

Loras nodded. "Then I suggest you think about how to fix whatever you've done before Morgan catches wind of it. Because if she does, it might not matter if you like or love her; she might not forgive you. Trust me, son. I've been married a long time, and I know a thing or two about women. They don't forget shit."

"Thank you. I'll keep that in mind."

"Good. Let's get you back to the house. It's early, and if you're smart you can take those two out to the zoo or something fun to make up for the lack of the bike ride."

Shaun never had a father to guide him. Was this what it would've been like if his father had been even half human? He remembered Morgan telling him these were her adoptive parents. He never realized how lucky a person could be finding a home filled with love, even when they're not blood.

As they made it to the Jeep, Shaun knew exactly what he needed to do. *Why hadn't I thought of this before? It's the perfect answer and will solve all the problems, now and in the future.*

"Are you okay?" Loras asked as he buckled up his seat belt.

I will be. No. We will be. I just have to put the new plan into action. "Yes sir, I am. I'm just thinking about all the things I want to do with Tyler and Morgan."

"Good. But today, the zoo is a good start. He loves to ride the elephant."

Excellent. Something we all can ride together.

Chapter Fifteen

MORGAN HAD A fantastic weekend with Shaun and Tyler. Her first thought when she saw her father talking to Shaun was that the romance was over. She knew that look on her father's face. He was upset and wouldn't share what was wrong, not even with her mother, which was out of character. Thankfully whatever it was, they solved it as both men had returned in one piece.

She sat at her desk, holding her phone and scrolling through the pictures. Tyler truly had a good time at the zoo. He would have ridden the elephant a hundred times if she'd allowed it. Ordinarily she just watched, but this time had been different. She found the picture she was looking for. She was in the front, Tyler in the middle, and Shaun in the back as they rode around on the great beast.

When he first said he wanted them all to ride together, she thought for sure he was joking or only doing it to humor Tyler. Looking at the picture now, she noticed Shaun looked as happy as her son.

"Who would've thought Shaun was just a big kid at heart?"

"I would have."

Morgan put her phone face down on her desk, embarrassed to have gotten caught playing at work. She recognized the voice because of the daily phone conferences she'd had. *Crap. Surprise personal appearance.*

"Hi, Tessa." Morgan got up and came out from behind her desk to shake her hand. "I'm Morgan. It's so nice to finally meet you in person."

"Please sit and relax. I didn't stop by to check on you. I'm actually meeting Dean for lunch. You and Shaun should join us."

Oh, no. We're not . . . well, I don't know what we are. But whatever it is, I like it. I like him. A lot. "I have a lot of work to finish."

"Morgan, I'm your boss, and I know exactly what you need to complete today. Do you think I was bored and just happened to find my way down here?"

She shook her head. *I actually thought you were checking up on me. Someone should. I've been here for weeks and only once did Shaun come down.* Morgan remembered exactly how that ended. *Kissing him until I thought I would die.*

"I didn't realize this was a business lunch."

"It's not. So we'll see you in the lobby at noon. No excuses." Tessa smiled and left Morgan alone once again.

There was a time she craved the solitude. Now, not so much. There was one companion she was missing terribly. *How is it that in just a few weeks he has me tied in knots?*

She picked her phone up again, and it was still on the picture of the three of them. It was what a family photo would look like. *If we were actually a family.*

Morgan tried not to overthink it, but she couldn't help herself. Like every young girl, she'd dreamed about finding her happily ever after. She knew that wasn't what she and Walter were about, but once Tyler came along she yearned for him to have a father in his life. *Having no father is better than one who treats you badly.*

She knew Tyler wouldn't be the loving boy he was if Walter had been around. Walter made everything and everyone around him tense. She could only imagine how much worse it would've been for the child to have endured his endless badgering. *We would've been yelling and fighting every day about what was best for Tyler. No, thank you. He didn't need that in his life. We're better off alone than living like that.*

It was sweet thinking she was no longer alone. They had Shaun in their lives. Not only did she spend Saturday with him, but he also came on Sunday. It wasn't the fast moving pace they'd had at the zoo, but at least, they were together. He even stayed while she got Tyler ready for bed. At first she thought it was because he wanted to spend the night, but soon after Tyler was asleep, Shaun kissed her and went home.

Had spending the entire day with them two days in a row been too much? For someone who doesn't have children, it could have been overwhelming. *He's my son, and there're times I can't do it and need a break. It was probably more than Shaun expected.*

She looked at the clock. It was almost time to meet them. *Why did I agree? I am comfortable with Shaun, but I'm not ready to do lunch with his family.* There was no way she could call and back out now. Not only were they all her supervisors, but it was clear backing out wasn't an option earlier, so she doubted it'd be now.

Grabbing her purse, she left her office and made her way to the lobby. She was going to be early, but the last thing she wanted was the three of them waiting for her.

While Morgan waited, someone outside caught her attention. There was a man who looked familiar hanging around just outside the entrance. *Where do I know him from? I know I've seen him before, but where?*

Morgan remembered faces from her coffeehouse days, but that wasn't the case. This was much more recent. She got up and walked closer to the glass. It was the type you could see out, but not in. *Perfect for spying on someone.*

She normally wasn't bold enough to gawk at someone, but she had a strange feeling about him, and it wasn't good. As HR, she should be concerned about someone loitering around that might bring harm. *This day and age you can't be too careful.*

Her heart almost leaped from her chest. She remembered where. *I saw him in my neighborhood.* She looked around to see if anyone else had noticed him. No, it was just her and the security guard at the moment. Morgan debated asking the guard to go out and check him out. Find out who the man was, what he was doing there, but what if it was just her imagination? She looked at her watch again. It was ten minutes before noon. *Okay. I need to know if I'm right or if I'm losing my mind.*

She walked to the door and left the building. It wasn't going to be a long walk. Just long enough to make it appear she was leaving. If he followed her, then she had her answer.

Briskly she walked down to the sidewalk and crossed the street at the crosswalk. Making her way to the ice cream stand, she decided to order something just to act normal. This would give her enough time to adjust herself to look around at her surroundings and see if he was anywhere nearby.

Shit! Although her gut said she was being watched, she now had proof. The man was by the magazine rack right across the street. *Why? What could he want with me? It can't be about work because I'm nobody important. For him to be around my house and here, he's got to be a pervert or some stalker. But why me?* She couldn't stand there contemplating the answer.

Her hands trembled as she paid the man for the ice cream. She took it and headed back to Poly-Shyn. *Maybe checking on this alone wasn't a wise decision. Come on, move these feet faster and get your butt back to work where you are safe.* When she passed a trashcan, she slipped the untouched cone inside. Not waiting for the crosswalk, she bolted across the street. Car horns blared, but she didn't care. Right now she needed to get back to talk to Shaun. She had to tell him.

Morgan dug in her purse while walking briskly. *Damn. I forgot my cell phone on my desk. Great!* One more block and she'd be there. From where she was she could already see the limo parked in front, waiting. *Almost there. Keep moving.*

When she arrived at the limo, she peeked inside, but there was just the driver. That meant they were still inside the building. She ran through the automatic glass doors and found Shaun, Dean, and Tessa standing there.

He must've seen the fear in her eyes because he was by her side with his arm around her instantly. "Baby, what's the matter? What happened?"

She was trying to catch her breath. "Shaun, I wasn't imagining it. It's real."

He brushed a stray hair away from her face and asked, "What's real?"

Morgan forgot. She'd never told him of her suspicions. *No time like the present.* "I'm being followed."

Shaun looked around then turned back to her. "Why do you think that?"

"There's a man outside wearing a baseball cap who I've seen lurking around my house. Now he's here at my job. I don't believe in coincidences."

"Are you sure he's the same man?"

"Yes. When I noticed him, I went for a walk two blocks down the street and even crossed the street to make sure. He followed me there and then followed me back." She pointed to the man she was talking about. "See. He's right there. Acting like he's reading, but in fact, he's watching."

"Oh my God, Morgan. That's horrible," Tessa said.

"No one would want me, but I know one person who'd be crazy enough to do something to Tyler." Her blood boiled just thinking of him. "Walter Sapp, Tyler's father."

"Morgan, it's not Walter having you followed. It's me," Shaun said while still holding her.

She looked up at him puzzled, hoping she'd misunderstood. The look in his eyes said she hadn't. "What do you mean you're having me followed?"

He eased his grip on her but didn't let go fully. "They're people I hired to keep an eye on you and Tyler."

She pushed away from him. "Why?"

"Because I don't trust Walter any more than you do."

"And you didn't tell her about it?" Tessa interrupted.

Morgan appreciated Tessa's support, but that didn't change a thing. Was that why Shaun was spending so much time around them lately? She'd hoped it was because he'd come to care for them. She couldn't bring herself to voice her thoughts because she knew the answer. Her heart was breaking, and it was Shaun's fault. "I'm sorry. I need to go."

Shaun grabbed her arm as she tried to leave. "Wait. I

want to explain."

She looked at his hand and said harshly, "Let go of me. And I don't want to ever see you again. Do you understand? Never again!"

Although she knew her angry words were harsh, she couldn't stop herself from voicing them. Pain and betrayal had bubbled over. Not only was she upset with him, but with herself for putting herself in the situation in the first place. *I knew it. What was I thinking opening myself up like that?*

His fingers slowly released her, and she headed through the glass doors. Tears of anger streamed down her cheeks. *How could you do this to me? To us? I know you might think you were doing the right thing. You were trying to protect me and my son, but you should have told me what was going on. Let me decide what to do. All I wanted was your love, but you couldn't give that, could you? No all you could give me was manipulation to try to control me. Thanks, but I've had enough of that already. I was looking for so much more, something real.*

She needed to get home. When she told her parents what Shaun had done, she knew they'd be furious with him. *Dad won't be all smiles with you after this. Actually, I think you might be the person he hates second most in this world.*

Within minutes, she hopped on the public transit and was making her way to where she'd parked her car. *I need to stop working in Boston. It obviously doesn't agree with me.*

"WHAT THE FUCK was that about, Shaun?"

"My words exactly, well almost," Tessa said, giving Dean a warning look to watch his language. "Might as well practice now. I don't want you swearing in front of the baby."

Shaun normally enjoyed watching Dean get put in his place, but right now he was too pissed at Bennett to care. "I have Bennett and his men watching her and Tyler."

"Why?" Dean had a look of shock on his face no different than Tessa.

Dean, do we really need to do this in front of Tessa? She's going to tell Zoey, who will, in turn, tell Lena, and then I'll have to hear it from Brice. "It's complicated."

"Isn't it always with the Henderson men?" Tessa stated.

You don't know the half of it. Oh wait, yes you do because you almost got killed because of Dean. "Remember her former employer?"

"WS & Son? Yeah. They really don't like her. You said there was no issue there. Were you wrong?" Dean asked.

"No. The son is Tyler's father. Let's just say their family is a bunch of bastards. Do you know that Tyler is autistic?"

They both shook their head. "What does that have to do with anything?" Tessa asked.

"When his father and his family found out they didn't want anything to do with him. They weren't there for him emotional or financially. And not only that, they worked to make sure she never got another job in the field again. They purposely set out to ruin her. The sad thing is she never went after them for anything. Not one penny. She didn't even collect unemployment when she left. Morgan decided to do it all on her own."

"She certainly sounds amazing. But that doesn't explain why you had her followed."

Oh, sweet Tessa. Don't you know by now that Hendersons fuck up everything they touch? "It was time someone taught that family a lesson."

Dean raised a brow and asked, "Is that why their stocks are dropping faster than they can recoup?"

"Yes."

"Shaun. That's a dangerous game to play. I mean I do that shit all the time to acquire a company, but you're making this personal. The one who has something to lose doesn't seem to know what you're doing either."

"I made sure not to link her to what I was doing. But just in case, I hired Bennett to keep a close eye. I thought he was better than slipping up like this." Shaun planned on given Bennett a piece of his mind when he saw him next. But right now he had bigger things to worry about, and that was fixing things with Morgan.

"It really doesn't sound like Bennett. His men don't make mistakes like that." Dean's face showed concern as he spoke.

Shaun had no issue calling Bennett out on what happened in front of Dean. He might like the guy because he saved their lives, but right now he sucked.

Pulling out his cell, he dialed Bennett's number.

"What's up?"

"Your lackey screwed up."

"Care to give me a bit more information, Shaun, or did you call just to blow off steam?"

"Bennett, your guy got made. And not by me, but by Morgan. Great job."

"My guys don't make that kind of mistakes."

"Listen, you cocky bastard. I saw him myself right outside of the office building so don't tell me what they do and don't do." Shaun didn't want to hear excuses. Bennett's mistake may have just cost him Morgan.

"Shaun, I don't have any men at Poly-Shyn. If you're serious, I need a full description now, and I'll alert the team."

Fuck. "Double up, Bennett. I think the guy knows he was made, and if he's not yours, she could be in trouble."

"Where is she?" Bennett demanded.

"I don't know. Going home I guess."

"Wait, let me track her phone."

I hate that it's possible to do such things. But right now, thank God for advanced technology with remote tracking. He needed to know she was safe. That was why he started all this. And now it was blowing up in the worse possible way.

"Shaun, her phone is in the building. Are you sure she left?" Bennett updated him.

"Yes. We saw her walk out of here about ten minutes

ago."

"I'll get some men over to the house and also have them scope out the neighborhood for that guy. Text me what he looked like, and I'll blast it out. Until we know who he is, I think you should also have someone close by."

"I don't need any fucking babysitter, Bennett. Just find her and keep her safe. Understood?"

"Roger that."

"Shaun, find her, and then tell her you love her," Tessa said.

Love her? Who said I love her? I'm just worried about her and Tyler; that's all. He turned to Dean. "We are all on alert until we hear back from Bennett."

"Agreed. Now go find her, Shaun."

Shaun nodded, headed out the door, and hopped in the waiting limo. He dialed Loras's number and gave him the heads-up on what was coming.

"She's not home yet, but I'll text you once she arrives," Loras said before disconnecting the call.

The limo darted between traffic heading to her house. He'd never before felt such panic. Not even when Dean was going after Tessa. Could Tessa be right? Could this be love? He had nothing to compare it to, but whatever it was, caused him physical pain. It was like a knife in his chest. *She's okay. She has to be. Morgan, just go home where you belong. And so help me God, if anything happens to you or Tyler, I will kill the bastard with my bare hands.*

Chapter Sixteen

MORGAN SLAMMED THE car into park and made a mad dash for the house. The entire way home she cursed Shaun in her head. He'd hurt her, and she'd never forgive him for that.

Her father was standing on the porch when she got there. By the look on his face he wanted to talk. She didn't. "Not now, Dad."

"Yes, Morgan. Now."

She looked up at him. "You have no idea what Shaun did. Trust me, if you had any clue you'd—"

"I know, Morgan. I already knew. Now get in the house where you're safe," Loras said, and she saw him looking past her as though watching for something.

"Dad, Shaun's men can watch me all they want. He might be a jerk, but he'd never let anyone hurt me."

Her father looked at her as he said, "That wasn't one of his men. So until he gets here and we figure out what really is going on, you stay inside." He opened the front door and waited for her to go inside.

Thirty-six and still treating me like a little girl. You're lucky I love you so darn much, or I'd tell you no. She'd never disrespected her parents, and she wasn't about to start now. She trotted past her father and went to sit in the living room. Plopping herself into the overstuffed lounge chair, she let out a heavy sigh.

"Oh dear, you look like you've been crying," Elisabeth said as she entered the room.

Yep. All the way on the train and the drive here. I must look like hell. I know I feel like it. "I'm better now. Just needed to get it out of my system."

"I don't blame you after what Walter did."

"I wasn't crying over Walter." *Why would I? He's nothing to me, to us. He's out of our lives and can't hurt me. Unlike Shaun Henderson.*

How she wished that was the truth. No matter what, Walter's lack of interest in Tyler did hurt her. If it didn't, she wouldn't be human. But it was a different kind of pain than what she was feeling right now. *I never loved Walter, but I did love Shaun. Damn . . . I do love Shaun.*

It was a realization she wished she didn't need to face. It was past. She loved him, but that was before she found out he wasn't around her for the reasons she'd thought. *Oh God. I even made love to the man. How could he bring me to his house and . . .* Tears started coming down all over again. *Why Shaun? What did I do to you that made you do this? Did you trust me so little that you had me watched like this? Couldn't you have just asked me what you wanted to know? I would've told you. But no. You needed to hire people to watch and report back. I feel so. . .*

so violated.

Elisabeth came over and wrapped her arms around her. "There. There. It's okay. Shaun will be here soon, and you'll see, everything will be okay."

He's coming here. No. "I don't want to see him, Mom." It was too soon for her to be able to have an adult conversation. Her emotions were all mixed up right now and crying in front of him was only going to let him know that he'd won. *And I don't want him to know how much I care. He's not going to get the last laugh on me.*

She heard her father coming into the house, speaking to someone. The voice wasn't Shaun's.

"Morgan, this is Bennett. He works for Shaun."

I don't want to meet anyone associated with him. Not a friend, not family, and not someone who works for him doing God knows what. "Are you one of his goons spying on me?"

"We are providing security, yes."

Hmm. Security. Funny. I'm not at risk. Unless you consider Shaun ripping my heart from my chest and walking all over it a risk. "I don't want or need it."

"I would like to think so, but from what we see, you do."

"Really? Good, then when Shaun gets here I want you to protect me from that jerk." Morgan got up; she couldn't just sit back and let them all control her life, her actions. That is exactly what Shaun did when he hired people to watch her. He took away her rights. Her freedom.

"If need be, I would, but he's no threat to you, Morgan. He has never been." Bennett stood, blocking her from leaving the room.

"You don't know him." *I never would've thought he was capable of this either.* "He is having you watch me for no good reason."

"I wouldn't say that, Morgan. But I will let him explain to you what the driving force behind his actions is."

There was nothing Shaun could say that would ever make her feel his actions were justified. *Not telling me what you were doing is no different than lying to me.* No way was she going to open herself up to him so he could hurt her a second time. *Once is more than I can bear.*

"I have already told him I never want to see him again, and I meant it."

"I can't do that," Shaun's voice chimed in from behind Bennett.

"I'll be on the porch if you need me," Bennett said as he excused himself from the room.

"You can go with him now, Shaun. I don't want to hear anything you have to say." Morgan didn't care that she was about to air her dirty laundry in front of her parents. She had nothing to be ashamed of. *Falling in love with someone under false pretense makes me the victim. Letting you back into my life would make me a fool. And I'm no fool, Shaun Henderson.*

"Morgan, I want you to sit and listen. After you hear what he has to say, then you decide what you want to do," Loras said.

Has everyone gone crazy? Why does everyone think I need to hear anything he has to say? What if he lies to me? What if I believe the lies and he only hurts me again later? I can't risk it. It'll hurt too much. I already cut it off. Better to keep it that way.

"Dad, you're supposed to be on my side. Why are you standing by Shaun?"

"Maybe because what he has to say is something I wanted to do for a long time. Not the way he did it, but trust me, Morgan, I've felt the same damn way ever since that bastard decided he didn't wa—"

"Loras. Don't forget we have little ears listening, and we don't want that ever said in this house," Elisabeth reminded Loras, and everyone else as well.

Tyler was very attuned to what was said and picked up on everyone's emotions. Morgan should've remembered that earlier as she spoke to Bennett. Since it seemed all was quiet in the kitchen, she hoped he had his headphones on listening to one of his DVDs instead of their arguing.

The last thing she wanted was her son to be hurt. Right now he hadn't been affected. She wanted to keep it that way. "Shaun, this is just another reason why we shouldn't talk."

"No. That's a reason why we should speak quietly."

Don't play games. You know I don't want to see you, so why force it? There are a million women who would love to be with you. Go find one of them and leave me alone. "I don't need to come up with any reason, because I don't want to talk to you."

"Your father even knows we need to talk. So stop being stubborn and sit and listen."

She looked at him then her father. *I hope you're happy, Dad. This is not what I want, but I don't seem to have a choice now, do I?*

"Fine. Say what you want to say, then you can go and leave Tyler and me alone." *Just like we were before we met you.*

SHAUN KNEW SHE was pissed off. He was the one to tell her, but how it came about was wrong. How was she ever going to trust him again? He'd kept something huge from her, and no amount of apologizing was going to change that.

"Morgan, what I did was not to hurt you, but to help you and Tyler."

"Bull," Morgan said plainly, meeting his gaze. Her normally sweet honey brown eyes were dark and filled with anger.

"When I found out what Walter did, how he . . . walked away from his responsibilities, I wanted to teach him a lesson. One he'd never forget." *Crush him, make him wish he'd never been born. Not going to tell you that.*

Morgan looked at him long and hard. He wished he could read her thoughts, but from her expression he wasn't sure he wanted to know.

"I don't remember telling you about that. How did you know? Did you have me investigated?"

And this is getting worse. Why didn't I listen to Bennett? Oh, because I don't listen to anyone. And look at me now. I'm kicking myself in the ass and hoping she'll understand why I did it.

"Standard procedure with a new hire."

"I might be new in HR, but that type of information isn't included in a background check. Want to try again or is lying what you do best?"

No one had ever called him a liar. What he did wasn't lying as far as he was concerned. It was withholding information which was totally different. "We had some concerns with our contract division. Someone was altering them without Dean's or my recommendations."

"What I did was an improvement. Not something to cause concern," she said, trying to defend herself.

"Any form of tampering is a concern to us. You have no idea what this family went through last year. Tessa was kidnapped, and Dean was shot because of an employee tampering with the business. So don't tell me when it's appropriate to protect people you care about and when it's not."

Morgan nodded. "Sorry. I forgot about that. I can see why you might need to go to extreme levels of security now. But did you honestly think I was going to do any harm then? Or now for that matter?"

"At first, I honestly had no idea what to think. You walk off the street and into a job with more access than I ever would've granted you. But it hadn't been my decision. If it had been, you wouldn't have gotten the job."

"Thanks for the honesty."

"Tell me you'd have done things differently." Shaun challenged her, knowing full well how she'd answer. He knew Morgan was responsible, and she never would've turned over such information without checking out the person fully. Of course, some questions had been unprofessional; that was only because of the roadblocks they'd encountered.

"You're right. If I were in your shoes, I wouldn't have hired me either. But that doesn't explain what this has to do with Walter."

"We found out that he was blackballing you, so you would never be able to get a job in contracts again. That's not the only thing he didn't want. Well, you know. But he wanted you to suffer. For what reason I wasn't able to find out, but to me, it didn't matter. I only needed to know he wanted to hurt you. And from there, I was going to hurt him more than he ever thought possible."

"You should've told me and let me tell you how I felt, let me decide what action to take. But instead, you pulled all control away from me. You made this about you and not about Tyler and me."

"You're too damn nice and never would've retaliated."

"So your explanation is you did this behind my back because you think I wouldn't have wanted it. Am I correct?"

Shit, she's good. There's no answer I can give that won't make me sound like the asshole I am. "Yes."

He could see she was trying to process all the information he had thrown at her. When she finally spoke, the anger was gone, replaced with pain. And not just pain from learning what Walter had been doing, but more importantly what he'd done to her. Everything in him wanted to pull her into his arms and kiss her until she forgave him. Truth was, he knew this was going to take more than that to get her to trust him again. *I am a jerk. A straight up jerk. I could've handled this so many different ways, but I chose to do this my way. Ignoring how she was going to feel when she found out. Yep. Total jerk.*

"I can't stay here talking about this right now. I need to be alone." Morgan got up and headed for the doorway leading to her apartment.

He heard her sob as she turned the corner. *Damn it. I made her cry. I never wanted to hurt you.* "Morgan," he called out to her, but she didn't respond.

He started to follow Morgan but Loras stopped him, giving him a pat on the back. "Give her time, Shaun. She'll come to her senses. Right now she only sees one thing."

"What's that?"

"The pain. You broke her heart, Shaun. Now if you love her, you'll give her space to heal and then try talking to her again," Elisabeth said. "I know how much she cares about you. Just give her time and it will be okay."

Patience. Understanding. Neither is my strength. But

for Morgan, I'll do anything.

"I have someone I need to go and see right now."

"Walter?" Loras asked as Shaun headed for the door.

"Yes. No matter what Morgan thinks, I will not let that man hurt her or Tyler." It was the only thing he knew to be true. *Even, if she doesn't believe me.*

"Would you mind some company? I have a few things I would like to say myself," Loras said as he grabbed his hat from the banister.

Shaun looked at him. The last thing he needed was something happening to her father. She'd never forgive him. *Hell, I wouldn't forgive myself.* "Loras, we don't know what we're walking into. If he's having her watched, we are going to need to make a point in a way you might not want your name associated with."

"And you do?"

"Hendersons aren't known for being or playing nice. I'll only be upholding the family reputation."

"Then I positively think you need me, because if I'm right, my daughter is going to come to her senses, and it'll be nice if you're not in jail when she does."

Having him with them was going to change how they handled things, but maybe it was time for a change. *If I plan on being any part of her and Tyler's life, I can't keep being an asshole one hundred percent of the time. Maybe only fifty percent.*

"Okay, but stay close to Bennett. I want all of us walking out of there in one piece."

"So you have a plan?"

Not exactly. But I'll work on it on the way. "It's coming together."

Loras kissed Elisabeth goodbye. Before Shaun made it out the door, Elisabeth came up to him and gave him a hug and kiss on the cheek. "Don't do anything foolish, Shaun. They need you. Just remember that."

Is this what it feels like to have normal loving parents? They worry about your wellbeing and emotional state? He wasn't sure how to process it, but he knew it felt good. "I won't forget."

Walking to the limo, Bennett and two of his men joined them. Bennett explained they had four men watching the house now, and no one was going to get close to them at all.

"Thank you," Loras said. "They're all that matters to me."

Me too, Loras. Me too.

Chapter Seventeen

THEY WERE ALMOST at WS & Son when Loras broke the tense silence.

"Shaun, I think I hate that man as much as you, but I think we need to step back and think about what the long-term solution is."

"Putting him out of business so he has no funds to harass Morgan and Tyler ever again."

"You think you need money to be a creep? If only that were true."

Loras had a point. Broke or rich, that man was scum. *Maybe even more so without cash.* Something had to be done to stop him, but what?

"Loras is right. You are reacting to the situation. I'll back you with whatever you decide to do, within reason, but I would suggest thinking this through first," Bennett interjected as the limo veered off the highway and entered the exit ramp.

He knew he had their support, but what he needed right now was a good plan. Going into the company and beating the shit out of Walter sounded great at the moment, but Loras was right. The injury would heal, and Walter would be back with a vengeance. *Fuck. I can't let this keep going on, but I can't risk making it any worse either.*

Everything happening between him and Morgan was clouding his judgment right now. Even Loras was personally impacted by what was going down. He needed someone impartial to consult and advise him on the appropriate move. Someone who could look at the facts and devise a plan that wouldn't cause the people he loved more pain.

Love. When did I start loving them? That's not part of who I am. I don't love; I protect. Maybe that's all it is. I want to protect them. Yes. Protect them because I love them.

"Pull over," Shaun said to the driver as they made their way through the streets of Boston.

Once stopped, he turned to Bennett. "You know everything I do. But tell me what I don't know."

Bennett looked at Loras then back to Shaun. "We don't know if this guy Morgan saw is truly someone Walter has sent or not."

"Who else could it be?"

"The world is filled with creeps, Shaun, not just Walter. I say let my guys pick him up and see what they can find out. If it's one of Walter's guys, then we need to know what he wants from them. Is he doing it because he cares about them? Does he want to keep track of his son? Does he love her and want her back?"

It took every ounce of control not to reach across and

shut Bennett's mouth with his fist. Shaun didn't want to think about Walter in their lives at all, never mind moving forward as a family, as a father. *There's room for only one person in that role, and that spot is not Walter's.*

"Give your guys the go ahead." He needed to know who was behind this. Right now he wasn't sure if he was hoping it was Walter or not. If it wasn't, then he had more than one fish to fry. *I don't care how many people I have to deal with. If it takes an entire army, I'll hire them to protect Morgan. This I give my word on.*

Bennett turned to his guys. "Let's pick him up. Get me what I need."

The two guys sitting beside Bennett sat without any emotion on their faces. Shaun could tell they were on alert and ready to follow Bennett into anything. He wasn't used to such loyalty from staff. It was as though they were much more than just employees. He knew Bennett had served in the military before. *Maybe that's the comradery I see. Like family even though they're not.*

Everything kept coming back to the word *family*. He'd spent his entire life not relating to it, but now it seemed to be all he saw. *And all I want. I want Morgan and Tyler as my family. Now all I have to do is figure out how to make that happen. It would've been so much easier to accomplish when she was still speaking to me.*

"Loras, I need some advice. I have an idea, but I would like to do it without talking to Morgan."

"Oh, son. You haven't recovered from the last time you did that. Why don't you tell me what you're thinking? I'll be honest with my advice."

Shaun could work with that. "We all agree Walter needs to be out of their lives forever."

"You're not going to kill him are you?"

Tempting. Very tempting. "No. Right now his company is crumbling quickly. I think you and I should meet with him and use it in our favor."

"Not following you, Shaun."

"What is the one thing the Sapp family loves?"

"Money."

"Exactly. And what's the one thing we want?"

"Him out of Tyler's life for good."

"Do you know a good family attorney? I think it's time to draw up some paperwork for good ole Walter to sign."

"What type of paperwork?"

Shaun smiled. "One relinquishing all parental rights."

"And he's going to sign this why?"

"Because I'll take everything he has if he doesn't. If he does, I'll pull the sanctions we have in place. He'll recover over time."

Loras shook his head. "Remind me never to piss you off. You don't play nice."

He nodded. "I protect the ones I love, Loras. And I love your daughter and Tyler. So what do you think? While Bennett handles his stuff, do you want to come see a lawyer with me?"

Loras was smiling as he reached out his right hand.

"Count me in, son. I want to see that bastard's face when he realizes he's not the biggest fish in the sea any longer."

Bennett and his guys hopped out of the limo to handle their business. "Don't go see Walter without us, Shaun."

Don't worry. I'll take all the backing I can get to help the Sapp family see their options are limited. "I want this done before the end of the day. So you line up things on your end, and I'll get the forms needed."

"We'll rendezvous again at sixteen hundred hours outside of WS & Son."

Loras and Shaun spent the next two hours getting all the documents needed as well as pulling some strings with a judge so the paperwork would be processed immediately once it was signed. Shaun wasn't leaving any room for error this time. He needed to pull in a lot of favors with the Barringtons, but once they knew what the stakes were, they used their influence as well to make it all happen. *Sometimes it is all in who you know.*

He had prided himself in never needing anyone. He had his routine, and until Morgan came into his life, he never saw a reason to change it. His personal life was just that. In the last month, he'd been forced to share more of himself than ever before. It never became easier for him, but the reasons behind doing so did. *Anything for you, Morgan.*

On the ride to meet up with Bennett, Shaun made a quick call to Trent.

"There's been a change of plans, Trent."

"Do you want to buy the company instead of crushing it?"

"Hell, no. I'm going to use it as leverage for a deal I need him to take. If he goes for it, I'll need you to pull back so they can rebuild what they've lost."

"That's not going to be easy for them to do at this point. You said crush and that is one of my specialties."

He'd known that when he'd asked Trent for his help. How Walter was going to able to save his company was not his issue. He was going to give him the chance to rebuild, but that was all he'd promise to do.

"This woman sure must be special to you to have just thrown away millions of dollars on something you're not even going through with."

You don't know the half of it. "I'm meeting with the Sapps in ten minutes. We should know shortly what, if anything, needs to be done."

"I'll be ready, just say the word."

"Thanks, Trent, I owe you."

Bennett's team pulled up behind the limo, and he and his men got inside.

"What did you find out?"

"The stalker guy won't be bothering her again."

"One of Walters's men?"

"No. A regular pervert off the street. Trust me. He won't be anywhere near her again."

One down. One to go. "Good. Let's get this show on the road."

Shaun, Loras, Bennett, and his two men entered the

building. The man at the security desk looked like he was about to shit his pants. *Yeah. I wouldn't want to have to say no to us either.*

"Call your boss. Tell him Shaun Henderson wants to meet with him now."

The man dialed the number and mumbled into the phone. "Sorry, his secretary said they're in a meeting."

"I don't care if he is meeting with the President himself. If he doesn't meet with us in the next five minutes, he won't have a company to meet about."

The guard looked past Shaun and to Bennett and his men. He swallowed hard and picked up the phone again. It was apparent he was delivering a message that was going to cost him his job one way or another. *Sorry buddy, you're just collateral damage.*

"He'll see you. I can show you to the conference room. Please follow me."

When they went through the double doors, the alarm beeped. The guard turned back and said, "That's the metal detector."

"We know," Bennett said but made no effort to remove his weapon. "I believe you were showing us to the conference room."

The guy nodded, and with his head down, he hurried to the conference room and showed them inside. "They will be down shortly."

Once they were alone, Shaun looked at Bennett. "Was that wise?"

"Giving him my gun wouldn't have been. He'd

probably have shot himself in the foot or worse."

He shook his head. *You're a crazy bastard. Glad to have you with me.*

"With this group, I realize you really don't need me," Loras said, looking around the room.

"You're the one who's in charge of making sure I don't rip him to pieces."

Loras laughed. "I was going to offer to clean up the mess. Hope I can keep my cool when I see his dumb ass again. After what he put my baby girl and grandson through . . . it just isn't right. Not one bit."

Shaun saw the frustration and pain in the man's eyes. All those years he'd been powerless to fight against them and their money. It felt good to knock Walter down and have Loras standing there by his side when they delivered the message.

"He's getting his, Loras. You and I are making sure of that." He knew Loras needed to be involved. Shaun might love Morgan, but this man had been there all thirty-six years, fighting for her happiness. He wasn't about to steal the glory all for himself now.

The door opened and Walter Sapp, Senior and Junior entered with a few people meant to intimidate. It wasn't working. As soon as they saw Bennett, an entirely different feel entered the room.

There was an unspoken connection, felt and barely seen, but Shaun knew it was there. He'd seen the slight nod of Bennett's head to the man at Sapp's side, who seemed to be in charge. *A mutual respect? Or do these guys have a history as well?* From their stance, he went with the latter. *I hear once a Marine, always a Marine.*

The father spoke first. "I don't know who the hell you think you are, coming into my company and demanding to see us."

"I think we're the individuals crushing your company."

The son looked around the room, and his eyes stopped on Loras. "Do I know you?"

"Yeah, you stupid piece of shit. I'm Tyler's grandfather. You know, the son you don't acknowledge." His voice was filled with hate and accusations as he spoke.

"What do you want? What are you doing here?" Sapp Junior asked.

"Not what I want to do, but I'll settle for this." He pulled out paperwork from his back pocket.

"What is this?"

Shaun decided to take it from there. Loras had his turn, but now the business side was on him. "Legal documents stating you give up your parental rights to Tyler."

"And why would I do that?"

"Besides the fact that you don't want him?"

Sapp looked at Shaun then smiled. "I might not want him, but you do." He tossed the paperwork at Shaun. "And that's the only reason why I won't sign. You fucked with me, now I'll fuck with you. I want custody of my son. And trust me, I'll get it. His mother can't get a job other than serving coffee, and that's only because I allow it."

Shaun stepped forward, and Bennett grabbed his arm stopping him. *I'm going to kill that bastard. He's more hateful than we thought. He reminds me of my father, and that's not a good thing. Not one bit.*

"You think you scare me? You have no idea who I am, do you?" No one answered. "Then let me introduce myself. I'm Shaun Henderson. I'm sure you all remember my father, James Henderson?"

He enjoyed the look that father and son shared before turning their attention back to him. They nodded.

"Well, he taught me well. Your stocks are falling, and your company will cease to exist in about thirty-six hours. If you think stopping me will change anything, you're wrong. I have very influential friends who wouldn't be happy if anything happened to the people I love or to me."

"Your hired men don't scare me. I have my own," Sapp Senior said.

Shaun watched the men once again make eye contact with Bennett, yet there was no movement by either party. *You don't have shit. You just think you do.*

"Quite frankly, I was talking about my friends and family. I'm sure you know the Barringtons. Lovely family. Just don't fuck with them. Or, how about Trent Davis or Dax Marshall? Any of these on your friends list?" Silence once again. "Thought not. So are you ready to sit and sign?"

"What do we get in return?" Sapp Senior asked.

"I'll stop the destruction of WS & Son."

He turned to his son and said, "Walter sign the papers and get that bastard out of our lives."

Shaun knew it wasn't him they were talking about. Even with the company on the line, they couldn't see Tyler as anything more than an inconvenience. *You're the only bastards in the room.*

"No. We're not giving in to his threats, Dad. I'm not scared of him or any of his friends."

"Then you're a fool, son. I haven't worked my entire life to build this company so we can lose it because your ego is hurt. You don't want her, and you don't want the kid. You just can't stand losing. But if you don't sign the papers, I will be forced to remove you from everything I have. Is that understood?"

The two men stared at each other. The father wasn't going to back down. After a moment Sapp Junior picked up the papers, and as he was signing them said, "You can have him. Neither of them are worth my time."

As he was about to leave the room, Shaun turned and called out to him, "You better forget their names Sapp. Because if you continue to trash either of them, I will finish what I started, and your father won't be able to stop me. Am I understood?"

Sapp Junior glared at him and said, "You have your forms. What about my business?"

"You'll have your contracts and vendors back in place, if they choose to do business with you. I won't block any more of them."

Shaun left the room with Loras and the others close behind. Once they got into the limo, he texted Trent with the all clear. Then he placed another call to the judge for the paperwork to be processed. All they needed to do was stop by, and it would be finalized today.

"Shaun, what can I do to thank you for what you just did for my family?"

He looked at Loras. "You can give me your blessing to ask Morgan to marry me."

Loras looked shocked then grinning from ear to ear said, "Hot damn. Welcome to the family, son."

"Great. Keep that info to yourself for now." *All I have to do is get her to say yes.*

Chapter Eighteen

M ORGAN HAD SPENT the rest of the week going through the motions. She'd asked her father several times what happened when they went to see Walter, but he wouldn't tell her anything. He just kept whistling. The first few times she ignored it. Now it was driving her crazy.

It wasn't his fault, and she shouldn't take it out on him. He was happy, and she should be glad her father was so joyful. *So damn joyful it is making me sick. I don't want to see the sun come out. I don't want to hear the birds chirp or listen to love songs. I want to cry until my tear ducts close up and won't shed any more tears.*

She loved Shaun so much it was killing her not to see him. Yes, she told him she never wanted to see or hear from him again, but why did he have to listen? *He should've called, or sent flowers or come by and pulled me into his arms and begged me for forgiveness.* Yet none of it happened. Instead, she didn't go to work on Tuesday, and no one called to question it.

I can't believe he let me go so easily. It only proves I

don't mean that much to him and never did. She wouldn't compare him with Walter. No matter what happened, Shaun was a good man, and she knew it. The way he was with Tyler wasn't something he faked. He genuinely cared and that was what hurt the most. *Why couldn't you have been a jerk so I could hate you and move on? Now I have to suffer with the emptiness, and it is killing me.*

She picked up her phone and checked her messages. Nothing, no different than an hour ago. She could check every five minutes, but that didn't mean something was going to magically appear. Then she looked at her photos. *I should delete them, otherwise I'm going to look at them again and again. Do I like to torture myself with what will never be? Obviously I do because I can't stop looking at them. We were so close to having it all. Now, nothing.*

Morgan could hear Tyler playing in the other room. It wasn't going to be long before he would be waiting for their ride. Her heart wasn't going to be in it, no different than anything else, but she had to keep Tyler's routine as on track as possible.

This is not a weekend I'm looking forward to. She got up and looked out the window. She wanted to see Shaun's Jeep there, but it wasn't. There was no activity at all. Not Bennett or his men. Not even the weird guy with the baseball cap who'd been following her. *Out of sight, out of mind.*

"Tyler, time to put on your sneakers." *Come on Morgan, say it with some excitement. He's looking forward to it, so you better act like you are too.*

Tyler came into the living room with his sneakers in hand. He quickly put them on and was bolting out the door.

"Wait for Mommy," Morgan called after him but knew he wouldn't stop. Once he was focused on something, there was no getting his attention unless you were right in front of him.

She got up and headed downstairs. "Mom, we're heading out. We'll be back in an hour." Morgan had no idea why she informed her. The entire neighborhood knew when they left and when they returned. It was like clockwork.

"Wait for me. I want to see you off," Elisabeth shouted from the kitchen.

Ever since her fight with Shaun on Monday, her mother hovered over her like crazy. This was going a bit overboard. "You don't have to, Mom. I can get him settled myself." *I've been doing it for years. I don't need an audience.*

Morgan knew if she didn't wait, she would hear about it, so she stopped at the doorway but kept her eye on Tyler.

Elisabeth joined her and they headed to the garage. She noticed her father's truck was in the yard but he hadn't come in. *Maybe he's helping Tyler with his helmet. Thank God I have him and Mom. Don't know what I would do without them.*

She came around the corner and saw Tyler at the three-seater. "No Tyler. Not that one today." He kept pulling at it to get it to move. "Tyler, we don't need that one anymore."

"Why is that?"

She spun around to see Shaun standing by her father. "What are you doing here?"

"It's ten. Time for Tyler's bike ride."

She couldn't take her eyes off him. He was so calm and casual, as though nothing had happened. Morgan knew she felt and looked like it was hell-week in boot camp. "I know what time it is Shaun, but what I don't know is why you're here."

He walked over to her carrying some papers in his hand. *If this is termination paperwork, don't bother. I already quit when I stopped showing up.*

"I have something you might want."

"I don't want anything from you, Shaun." *Except your undying love. Which I don't have.*

"Morgan, listen to the man."

Morgan was startled as Loras barked at her. In all her life she didn't remember him ever raising his voice at her. *What's going on?*

"Fine. I'm listening." *Only because I have no choice in the matter.* Shaun approached her, and she stepped back. "I can hear you from here." She wasn't looking for an apology, but she was willing to stand there and listen if it made everyone feel better. She wasn't angry at him any longer. Part of her understood why he did it. Just one year ago Poly-Shyn was in an uproar after the shootings happened. *Business and pleasure don't mix for a reason.*

Mistakes are made and people get hurt.

"If Tyler wasn't here I'd—"

"What? Apologize?"

"Pick you up and carrying you off and make you listen to every word I have to say. And yes, that would include an apology."

She knew he was sorry. She was as well. Rehashing it wasn't going to help them move forward. Move on. And that was all there was left. *To move on.* "Shaun, you said enough last time you were here. What else is there to say?" She stood with her hands on her hips glaring at him.

"How about I love you."

Love me? You love me? She looked at her parents, who didn't seem at all surprised by any of this. "Is that what you wanted to hand me? A note professing your love?" No matter what he said, she still had her doubts after not one word from him for five days.

"Read it. It's something from both me and your father."

Morgan looked at Shaun then her father. "Just tell me."

"Read it," Loras said.

"Loras, give the girl a chance, will you? She hasn't even had a chance to process Shaun telling her he loves her," Elisabeth said, trying to be the voice of reason.

Thanks, Mom. At least someone understands. She took the papers from Shaun and read through them. Living in the world of contracts, she instantly was able to pick up the importance of what she held. *This can't be real. He'd never. Why would he? I mean I know he didn't want Tyler but what does it matter? I am doing it all on my own anyway.*

"I . . . I'm not sure why you are giving this to me. What does this change? I already knew he didn't want him, so this paper means what exactly?" She looked at both men for an explanation. Shaun was the one to provide it.

"It means that Tyler is free to be adopted at any time and have a real father in his life. One who loves him and will be there for him always."

I need to sit down. There is no way I'm hearing correctly. "Shaun what are you—?"

"I'm saying, Morgan, I want to marry you, and I want to be Tyler's father in every sense of the word. I don't want to wait to be asked to go on the bike ride, I want that seat to be mine. It is meant to be mine, Morgan, and you know it. You and me make three." He nodded over in Tyler's direction.

Hold it together Morgan. Don't cry because Tyler will get upset. No matter how she tried to hold her emotions, it was impossible. Tears of joy started gushing like never before. Not only had he professed his love for her, but for her son as well. There was nothing in this world he could give her greater than that. *He loves us with all our imperfections. And we love him with his too.*

That was when Morgan knew looking at the past was only going to hold them back from the true happiness waiting for them all in the future. *Time to take a leap of faith.*

Morgan jumped into his arms crying, "I love you too, Shaun. Yes, I'll marry you."

He kissed her lightly before they heard Tyler's voice shouting, "Shaun. Ride. Ride, Shaun."

Shaun released her and said, "We have the rest of our lives to finish this. But right now, our son is waiting for his bike ride."

Our son. She squeezed him one more time before letting go. They all put on their helmets and started down the driveway. She was smiling from ear to ear. *We're really a family.*

Epilogue

"I NOW PRONOUNCE you husband and wife. You may kiss your bride."

Shaun didn't need to be told twice. Even before the words had left the preacher's mouth, he'd claimed Morgan's.

"I love you, Mrs. Henderson," Shaun said as he released her slightly.

"I love you too, Mr. Henderson," Morgan said, encouraging him to kiss her again.

He smiled and gave her what she asked for but only briefly. Since they had chosen a very small intimate wedding in the backyard of her parent's home, their family had no issue interrupting the moment with hugs of congratulations. "Looks like we will need to finish this later," Shaun said. He let Morgan go as Zoey reached out to welcome her to the family. *Get used to it. Zoey is not shy in the least.*

Tessa's father had come from Connecticut to perform the ceremony. Dean was the best man, and her mother, Elisabeth, served as her matron of honor. Loras was the proud father as he walked her down the short aisle and insisted on paying for everything.

Shaun wanted to give Morgan the wedding of her dreams, a destination wedding anyplace in the world, but all she wanted was something simple. At first he didn't understand why, but as he stood among the people who truly meant something to them, it became clear. Morgan never was about show or status. What he loved about her was evident in her choices for the wedding. Love was all that mattered to her. And he loved her more than he could ever hope to express.

"Welcome to the family, Shaun," Elisabeth said as she kissed him on the cheek.

"Thank you, Elisabeth."

"Will you do me a favor?"

"Anything."

"You're the son I never had. I would love it if you would call me Mom."

Mom. His heart leaped into his throat. It was a name he was never allowed to utter before. One he had always wanted to. He might never know who his mother was or why she didn't want any of them, but as Morgan had told him before, family is not always who you are born to, but who chooses to love you.

"It would be an honor, Mom." He pulled her into his arms and hugged her tightly. "And may I ask a favor of you as well?"

"Anything."

"I have a surprise for Morgan. I want to give it to her

now. Will you forgive me if I steal her away for a few minutes?"

Elisabeth smiled at him. "As long as you remember to bring her back. We do have a cake to cut."

He nodded. "Thanks."

Shaun reached out for Morgan, who was still getting hugs from his family.

"I need my wife for a few minutes."

Lena laughed. "Are you kicking us out already?"

"No. We'll be back in ten." Then he turned to Elisabeth. "Mom, we are going to take Tyler too."

She smiled and nodded.

"Where are we going, Shaun?" Morgan asked, still glowing from the wedding kiss.

"Not far."

He went over and said to Tyler, "Mommy and I want to show you something. Can you come with us?"

Tyler reached his hand out to Morgan who took it in hers. Shaun could only hope that one day he might trust him enough to reach out to his. But baby steps were what she said, and they had grown so much already in only a few months.

As they left the backyard, they went down the front walkway and onto the sidewalk. Morgan headed to the limo that was parked out front, but Shaun shook his head.

"We are walking it."

She looked puzzled. "Okay."

He led them just a few houses down from where they

were. There was a house, which was similar to her parents, yet a bit larger and only a single family. Shaun pushed open the gate, and they walked onto the porch.

"Shaun, what are we doing here?"

He opened the door, which was unlocked, and ushered them inside. He watched her as she looked around the vacant living room before asking again.

"Shaun. What am I looking at?"

"Our new home."

"What do you mean? What about your place in Boston?"

"It is not a home, never was. And besides, it's not a place for Tyler to grow up. You taught me the importance of routine, and I have come to enjoy our weekend routine very much. Your father even agreed to let us keep the bikes at his house until Tyler gets used to them coming here."

Her eyes watered. "You really mean it? You're willing to give up all that luxury for this?"

"That stuffy, empty, lonely place where I showered and slept for a place I can look forward to coming home to each night? Maybe even get a home-cooked meal and a kiss at the door?"

She laughed. "I think I can arrange both. Dinner's at six."

That was something he already knew and planned on making as much as possible. "So you like it?"

"I love it. Thank you. Thank you for loving us the way you do."

He bent and kissed her gently. "No baby. I should be thanking you. Without you both in my life, I don't think I would even have a clue what love is."

She started to kiss him a second time, but he stopped her.

"I promised ten minutes, and I'm holding to it. We have the rest of our lives to make this our home." Then Shaun turned to Tyler and asked, "Tyler, are you ready for some cake?"

"Cake." He pulled Morgan's hand and headed back to Elisabeth and Loras's house.

Everyone was already standing around the cake when they arrived, and Elisabeth was holding a knife. She handed it to Shaun who cut the first piece, then he in turn handed it to Morgan. She placed it on the table without cutting into the cake.

"What's wrong?"

She leaned over and pointed at what was written on the cake. *You & Me Make Three.* He watched her cross out the three. Her hand was trembling as she took her finger and started writing in the frosting. F-O-U-R.

His stomach dropped. Was she saying what he thought she was? He grabbed her by her shoulders and turned her to face him.

"Are you?"

She nodded. "Yes, we are pregnant."

Shaun pulled her into his arms and hugged her so tight that he was afraid he may have hurt her. "Good thing I bought the five bedroom house. I was hoping you would want to fill it."

Morgan smiled. "I would love to."

As he kissed his new wife all he could think about was one day needing to build an addition to the home. Five bedrooms didn't seem anywhere close to what they would need. *Whether they will be born into the family or adopted, our family will fill this house with love.*

The End

Other books by Jeannette Winters

Betting on You Series:

Book 1: The Billionaire's Secret (FREE!)

Book 2: The Billionaire's Masquerade

Book 3: The Billionaire's Longshot

Book 4: The Billionaire's Jackpot

Book 5: All Bets Off

Barrington Billionaire Series:

Book 1: One White Lie

Book 2: Table For Two

Book 3: You and Me Make Three

Book 4: Virgin for the Fourth Time (Coming 2016)

Book 5: His for Five Nights (Coming 2017)

Book 6: After Six (Coming 2017)

Southern Desires Series:

Book 1: Southern Spice

Book 2: Southern Exposure (September 2016)

Book 3: Southern Delight (Coming 2016)

Book 4: Southern Regions (Coming 2016)

The Billionaire's Secret

Billionaire Jon Vinchi is a man with one passion: work. His friends decide to shake him up by entering him as a prize at a charity event.

Accountant Lizette Burke is dressed to the nines and covering for her boss at a charity event. She's hoping to land a donor for the struggling non-profit agency that employs her.

She never expected to win a date with a billionaire.

He never thought one night could turn his life upside down.

One lie stands between them and their happily ever after. Too bad it's a big one!

Available now!

One White Lie

Brice Henderson traded everything for power and success. His company was closing a deal that would cement his spot at the top. The last thing he needed was a distraction from the past.

Lena Razzi had spent years trying to forget Brice Henderson. When offered the opportunity of a lifetime, would she take the risk even if the price would be another broken heart?

Do you love reading from this world? Continue with Always Mine from my sister, Ruth Cardello, Her series will mirror my time line. It isn't necessary to read hers to enjoy mine, but it sure will enhance the fun!

Southern Spice

Derrick Nash knows the pain of loss. But is he seeking justice or revenge? He doesn't care as long as someone pays the price.

It is Casey Collin's duty at FEMA to help those in need when a natural disaster strikes. After a tornado hits Honeywell, she finds there are more problems than just storm damage. Will she follow company procedures or her heart?

Can Derrick move forward without the answers he's been searching for? Can Casey teach him how to trust again? Or will she need to face the fact that not every story has a happy ending?